HERO EVER AFTER

A NOVEL

SARAH READY

CROWN

W.W. CROWN BOOKS
An imprint of Swift & Lewis Publishing LLC
www.wwcrown.com

Copyright © 2020 by Sarah Ready
Cover by Mayhem Cover Creations
Published by W.W. Crown Books an Imprint of Swift & Lewis Publishing, LLC, Lowell, MI USA

Library of Congress Control Number: 2020925458
ISBN: 978-1-954007-04-8 (eBook)
ISBN: 978-1-954007-05-5 (pbk)
ISBN: 978-1-954007-06-2 (lg print)

SHE NEEDS A HERO. HE NEEDS A SECOND CHANCE.

Single mom Ginny Weaver needs a hero. Not an average hero. Not an everyday hero. A full-fledge, honest to goodness, super-duper A-list movie star, comic book action hero.

And she'll do anything to get one.

Liam Stone is a washed-up, has-been, former Hollywood superhero – now dubbed "the super zero".

He isn't what Ginny needs.

But Ginny's six year old daughter is sick and she has one last wish...

So, Ginny and Liam make a deal. Ginny will get a cape-wearing superhero for her daughter and Liam will get his chance at redemption.

But deals come with unexpected consequences, like questioning what really makes a hero, or a family, and whether or not love has anything to do with it.

Maybe, just maybe...love makes heroes of us all.

1

Ginny

I love heroes. Everything about them. Their strength, their honor, their devotion, their pursuit of the ultimate goal in the face of unsurmountable odds. A hero always does what's right, always wins, no matter what. Right now, more than anything in the whole wide world, I need a hero. I'm broke, widowed, a whisper from the edge, and my baby girl's dying—she wants a hero, and by all that's holy, I'll get her one. I'll get her the greatest superhero of all time. I'll get her Liam Stone.

I glance to the backseat of the car. Bean's strapped in her car seat. Her sixth birthday was last week and she's working through the pile of comic books that she got for her present.

"Do you think he'll lift a car?" she asks. "When he fought The Red Spider he lifted a car over his head and crushed him."

I take my eyes off the washed out dirt road and look in the rearview mirror. "I don't know, Bean. I don't know if retired superheroes still do that stuff."

Two lines pucker between her forehead as she thinks my answer over. "But he'll still train me?"

"If I have to wrestle him to the ground and force him."

She giggles and I nearly lose my breath at the happy sound.

"Mama, you can't beat Liam Stone. He's strong as two hundred men, quick as a rocket, and smarter than Einstein, aaand he's devoted to helping the misfortunate."

"Downtrodden," I say with a wry smile.

"He'll be happy to see me. I bet he's been wanting a protégé for years. All the best heroes have 'em."

I raise my eyebrows. Since when did she start using words like protégé? "You let me do the talking, Bean."

"I know." She buries her nose back in the comic book. I can barely see the top of her bald head over the bright cover of the comic.

I breathe through the pinch of panic that comes every time I see evidence of her being sick. Push it aside.

Anyway, we've made it. We're ten miles outside of Centreville where Route 511 crosses Route 511B and turns onto Pine Tree Road. Southern Ohio is full of fallow land sold for cheap, you can snatch up hundreds of acres, and be left alone for the rest of your life. Which is, I guess, what Liam Stone was hoping for. He bought the land two years ago when he *literally* fell from Hollywood stardom.

At first, everyone in town was starstruck, waiting for the day he'd come to Main Street so they could go gaga over him. But he never came. Two years on, no one in town has ever laid eyes on him. And no one has ever been brave enough to come out and introduce themselves—extend a neighborly hello. Nope, we've all just left him alone.

Until today.

I turn into his driveway and don't let myself think, because if I did I might back out.

I grip the steering wheel and my knuckles turn white. But I

keep my hold tight because if I relaxed I wouldn't be able to stop shaking. Please, please, please don't let me down. Please be a hero. Please be as good and kind and selfless as the character you played in the movies. I send out the prayer as we pass through the deep green summer woods of his land.

My car, old Bess, groans on the uneven gravel. Bless her, she keeps chugging along. The fabric on the ceiling sags, the stuffing of the seats sticks out, and the steering wheel's long faded from brown to gray, but she only breaks down every few weeks, which is better than my last car. Plus, a wrench, a few cuss words, and a swift kick are usually enough to restart her motor. I don't mind getting dirty if it means Bean still makes her appointments. Those are ninety miles away, too many days each week.

There's a wood fence on the side of the driveway. It's rotten and the tall grass swallows it. Finally, the woods open up and I pull to a stop at the end of the drive. The grass is weedy tall and there's a little trampled path to the front door. I park in front of the rusted trailer. It's a single wide. Baby blue and banana yellow with narrow little windows and a cement block patio.

"It looks abandoned," says Bean.

I shiver. It looks worse than abandoned, it looks like a horror movie. Maybe nobody ever met Liam Stone because he died two years ago and his body's been rotting in the squat trailer ever since.

But that can't be right. The FedEx guy says he drops deliveries from online grocery stores, and liquor distributors, and everything else under the sun, every single week. Somebody's getting those packages.

"It's not abandoned," I say.

I think I see a curtain flutter and I rub my hands up and down my arms. It's nearly ninety degrees, but darned if I'm not chilled.

Bean unbuckles her seat. "I bet he has his headquarters

beneath the trailer. It's a trick to fool The Red Spider." She grabs her red silk cape and starts to tie it around her neck.

As I wait for her to prepare, I look at the books piled on the passenger seat. *Overcoming Grief—A Widow's Guide. I'm Okay, You're Okay. The Single Mom's Guide to Motherhood. How to Let Go. Saying Goodbye. When Good People Die. Losing a Child.*

I clasp my hands and swallow back...everything.

Bean...

I shove all the books onto the floor. The pages flutter and they each hit the floor with a hard thud. They haven't been any help, none of them are any help.

"I'm ready, Mama," Bean says.

I turn to her. She's in her cape and mask. "Aren't you a picture. The best protégé a superhero could want."

She swallows and nods quickly. My fearless little girl is nervous.

I can't let her see that I am too. In all this, I never want her to see how terrified I am. That I can't handle it, that I'm so terrified that I stay awake at night, that I sob in the shower, that I have to force myself to eat, that I'm so scared for her. I can't let her see it. I need to be steady for her, so that she never knows that her mama is terrified for her. I have to be her rock, so that if the time comes, she won't be scared to go. When that time comes, after she's gone, then I'll fall apart. But until then, I'll stitch myself together and I'll hold it all in, so that not an inch of fear, or nerves, or stress shows through.

I open my door and step into the oppressive heat. I open Bean's door and she steps down into the gravel.

"I can't believe I get to meet Liam Stone," says Bean. "He's my hero, and I get to meet him. And I get to train with him. I'm the luckiest person in the world. Gran said that you don't know Liam Stone, and this was all going to end in *mountains of misery* and Heather said you're a failure and that Liam Stone is a laughingstock—"

"Well, Gran and Miss Heather—"

"But Finick said that Gran's mummified in her bitterness and Heather's a cold-hearted bi—"

"Beatrice Renae, we don't use that kind of language."

"I'm just repeating what I hear. They don't believe, but *I do* and so does Finick and you said you would do this and you always do what you say." She looks up at me with absolute trust and it nearly breaks me.

Because I learned real early that the worst part of motherhood, the worst part of life, is not being able to do anything. Not being able to save the one person you love more than yourself. I can't save my Bean. I can't kiss her and make her better. Nothing I do will stop her from hurting, dying. So instead, I'm going to give her the one thing she's always wanted.

A superhero.

She told me she had a wish. To train as a superhero under Liam Stone. And if I can get that for her, I will. I swear on my life and everything in me, I will.

Grandma Enid and Heather and all the other doubters, they don't know, they have no idea what I'll do for my child.

I take Bean's hand and feel the dry coolness of her skin. "Don't worry, Bean. Mr. Liam Stone won't be able to resist our charm. Besides, superheroes, even retired ones, always want to help others."

I glance at the rat-trap trailer, the tall grass and the unwelcoming atmosphere. "But maybe you could wait in the shade over there under that big oak tree. Just for a minute, while I chat with Mr. Stone. Alright?"

She looks me over, then at the trailer, then at the shade of the tree with the soft grass beneath it.

"I'll be quick," I say.

I give her a peck on her check and she scuttles off to lean against the wide oak tree. When she starts flipping through her comic I sigh and face the trailer with resolve. I walk up the overgrown path to the front door. There are thorns that scrape my bare legs and I kick the prickers back. Finally, I step on the concrete stairs and raise my fist. I knock hard and loud. This isn't the time for timidity.

Inside the trailer, I hear cussing, and glass bottles knocking over. He's in there, but after a minute, with still no answer I bang on the door again.

"Coming, coming. Hold your pants," a man shouts. His voice is booming and deep. I recognize it from seven block-buster films. The sort of voice that men wish they had and women wish was being whispered to them under bed sheets. Yes, that voice. Smooth, confident, rich and firm. The voice of a hero.

This'll be okay. Liam Stone may be living as a hermit in a dump in the middle of nowhere, but he's *Liam Stone*.

Cut muscles, eight-pack abs, shoulders to carry the world, brown eyes full of wisdom and empathy, a smile that warms the hearts of the worst cynic. This man was America's son, brother, husband and father all wrapped in one. He was our hero. He saved the world in the movies and then in real life he gave to charity and kissed babies. There's no way he won't want to help.

Also, *that voice*, it hasn't changed one bit.

I knock again, convinced that this is going to work. I'll get Bean her wish.

I lean against the door and knock again. Then the door's yanked open. I stumble and let out a sharp exhalation. I trip into the trailer and fall into a man's arms.

He jerks and pushes me back and away from him. I trip over the threshold and grab the door to steady myself.

"What the hell?" he says. "Who the hell are you?"

My mouth drops open and I stare at him in shock. This man...he's...he's...

Awful.

His bathrobe hangs open. Instead of an eight-pack he has a

gut. Instead of a clean-shaven jaw there's a scraggly beard. His hair is overlong and sticks up in every direction. His eyes are bloodshot and he smells like he just took a bath in cheap beer.

I look behind him and realize he did. The noise I heard earlier was him crashing through half-empty beer bottles.

"What. Do. You. Want." He looks me over, from the top of my ponytail, to my old tank, and my cut-off shorts, to my Vans shoes. His blatant perusal makes me feel like I'm the one in a ratty bathrobe and he's in a tux on the red carpet.

"Mr. Stone?" I ask.

His lip curls and I catch a hint of the snarl he used to give a villain right before he crushed them with his super strength.

"Unless you're here with my Lagavulin delivery, I suggest you get off my property."

He narrows his eyes and I see that he's about to slam the door. I catch the handle and put my foot in the entry.

"Wait," I say. "It's important I speak with you."

He pauses and nods slowly. "Ahh, I see. It's important."

"That's right," I say, my shoulders relax.

He smiles, and I catch my breath at that little hint of his charm. "In that case..." He lets go of the door and holds his hands out for me to come in.

Thank goodness. I can explain the situation, help him clean up the trailer, get him presentable for Bean.

I move my foot and let go of the door. I step back. "Thank you. You see, I—"

"Don't care," he snaps.

Then he slams the door.

"Hey!" He can't do that. He can't just—

I stare at the closed door.

He can't, but he *did*.

I hit the door. Kick it. Rattle the knob.

But Mr. Liam Stone doesn't answer.

He doesn't care. He doesn't even know and he still doesn't

care. A feeling of desperation claws at me and I vent it by pounding my fist against the rusty metal. He tricked me. He smiled at me, put me off my guard and then slammed the door in my face.

He's not a hero. He's awful. Awful.

I kick the door again.

I hear bottles being knocked about inside and a low curse.

He's a drunk. Bean's hero is a smelly, let-himself-go, rude, awful, drunk.

I drop my hand and my fingers clench into a tight fist. I have to hang on, I have to keep trying, except...I turn to go, because Liam Stone's not a hero. He's a villain.

2

Liam

*T*here's a hard knock at the door. It pounds through my skull and I groan.

"Go away." I pull a pillow over my head, but the infernal knocking doesn't stop. Each hit jackhammers through my skull and I flinch at the assault.

"Go the hell away."

But they don't.

So I finally push myself upright and stumble to the door. I decide to forgo the bathrobe. If the nuisance at the door wants to see me so badly, they can see me in my underwear. The room spins and I grab a table, then the wall. When I make it to the door I yank it open.

"What?" I glare into the bright sun. It hurts my head as much as the knocking.

"Mr. Stone." The voice doesn't match the huge fist I imagined banging on the door. I squint and my eyes adjust to the bright light.

"What," I say. Then I take in the woman. She's that expensive blonde type. Perfumed, designer dressed, high-heeled... Hollywood. I know her. Not her, precisely, but her type.

"Stoney," she says in a throaty purr, "you've let yourself go since I last saw you."

I narrow my eyes. Look her over again. Nope, don't know her. But she's looking at me like we...you know. But we didn't. Because I didn't mess around with women. I was in a relationship for my whole career and I didn't mess around.

She sighs. "It's Heather."

I look to the driveway at her car. It's a brand new Mercedes coupe. She's not the woman from earlier. I didn't catch much of the first woman, but she seemed a little more down to earth, plus she drove a rusty beater a few decades old.

I sigh and scrub at my face with my hands. "May I help you?"

Clearly the universe is out to get me. One day a year, just one, the same one for the past two years, I spend with as many bottles as it takes to *forget*. But for some reason, I'm not allowed to just pass out into oblivion so this day can roll by in a haze. No. Because people keep knocking on my door.

"I was in *The Red Lantern Returns*. Remember? After that I went on to daytime television." She goes on and talks about her roles, the shows, the movies, the life...I tune her out and think about climbing back in bed so this day can end. Then I realize she's stopped talking.

"Ah, what?" I ask.

Her upper lip curls. "I have a job offer," she says, more slowly than before.

I close my eyes and try to clear out the bowling balls that are knocking around my skull preventing me from thinking clearly.

"You'd have to get yourself cleaned up," she says. She lets her eyes linger on my scraggly beard, my stomach, my boxers. She gives a tight little smile and I have the urge to cover myself. "No booze, either." Her eyes flick to the row of beer bottles on the kitchen table. Shame prickles over my skin and I itch under the heat.

"All offers go through my agent," I say. I resist the urge to shift, to hide my shame. "You're talking summer blockbuster? Or a sequel?"

I've been waiting for this moment. For two years now. Maybe I was wrong and the universe is actually giving me a little good karma for once.

"A sequel?" she asks.

"An origin story then," I say. Those are big now, people love the superhero origin stories. If we do an origin story I won't have to fly. That's the hold up, I can't fly. Every time I think of strapping in and swooping through the air I break out in a cold sweat and can't breathe.

The blonde shakes her head. "Stoney. I'm not here for a movie. I want to hire you for a birthday party."

I stare at her, not quite comprehending what she's saying. "A what?"

"My son's turning eight. I want to hire you for the entertainment. Dress in your suit. Sign some autographs. Maybe do a few balloon animals."

The world fades and all I can see is this woman, one who apparently knew me before, asking me to be... "A clown? You want me to be a clown?"

"No," she says. She puts her manicured nails on my arm and I flinch. "A party entertainer. I'll pay you. A thousand dollars. It looks like you could the use the help, Stoney."

I step back. She's not here to convince me to come back to Hollywood, she's here to convince me to be a clown.

"Get off my property."

"A thousand dollars is a good rate. My son loves your

movies. Well, not loves, they're mediocre, but it's not like we could get Spiderman—"

"Get off my property."

Her eyebrows go high. "Really? What do you have to be so high and mighty about? Look at you." She waves her hands at me. "Look at you. Disgusting."

I don't need to look at me. I see myself in the mirror every day. I know it's not pretty.

"Get out of here," I say.

She spins on her heels and marches to her car. When she pulls out, her tires spin and kick dirt up as she fishtails down the gravel drive.

I slam the door.

My head aches and I want to climb back in bed and sleep away the rest of this day. But my agent called last week and it's high time I called him back.

I pull out my phone and text him, *you up for a call?*

In seconds my phone rings. I answer, aaand it's a video call.

Devon's face fills the screen, he's in a silk shirt and sunglasses, the Pacific Ocean's in the background.

"Liam. Good grief. Is that you? What have you done to yourself?"

I sigh. Yes, I gained twenty pounds. Sure, I don't have an eight-pack anymore. Yes, I look like crap. I get it.

"Good to see you too, Devon. You called last week?"

"Hmm. Did I? Let me see." He pulls out another phone and starts tapping through his notes. "Right. Here it is. I have a job offer."

I fight down the little blip of fear. I can do it. I can jump back in, do the stunts, take the risks, fly.

"Yeah?" I say, and my voice only cracks a little.

"Best offer you've had in years. Hemorrhoids."

"What?"

"Hemorrhoid commercial."

"They...you...what?"

"Liam. You don't look so hot. Let me book you for this. Take the week, clean yourself up. You can shoot on the twentieth. A clean twenty thousand, the usual percentages for representation."

"You want me to do a..."—I can't say it—"a commercial?"

"Buddy. It's not what I want. It's what the people want."

I've heard that line from Devon before, but it was when he was negotiating on my side for a multi-million-dollar movie role.

"I thought..." I clear my throat, start again. "It's been two years. I'm ready."

"Buddy. Look at you. You're not ready."

"It's been two years. Two. Years. How long can they blacklist me?" I stop when I see the distaste form on Devon's face.

I catch myself in the camera and I barely recognize the man I see. Pale, deep-lined skin, dark bags under bloodshot eyes, and hollow desperation. I turn away from myself and back to Devon.

"I'm better," I say firmly. "I'm ready."

Devon looks down at his watch, then back to me. He's done, he's already checked out from the conversation. He used to do the same move with D-list actors he didn't want to deal with. He'd look at his watch, say he had a meeting, that he'd get back to them later. After they'd left he'd laugh at how pathetic they were to believe him.

"Buddy, I've got a meeting. I'll get back to you later."

He reaches to hang up. *He's going to hang up on me.* I've hit bottom. I've really, truly hit bottom.

"Don't bull crap me, Devon. Tell it to me straight. Am I ever going to play Liam Stone again?"

Devon sighs and pulls down his sunglasses. "Okay, buddy. I didn't want to say. Not today at least."

Today. June 27. The day I fell thirty feet during filming and broke five vertebrae in my back. I was lucky. I lived.

This god-awful day is the day my career died. And in all other purposes, so did I.

"You're finished," says Devon.

"No more Liam Stone films?"

"No more films."

I look down at myself. The out-of-shape body, the ragged clothes. I knew it already, didn't I?

I rub a hand over my face and drag it across the stubble. "What about—"

"No."

"Or—"

"No."

"I could—"

"No. Buddy. You had two chances. You lost your shit during filming on both of them. Cost millions of dollars. Set back production schedules months. No one will hire you. You're a liability. No one wants a liability."

"Not even—"

"No."

I sit with it, this knowledge that it's over. I knew it though. I've known it for years. It's just been a slow, gradual, painful slide to the bottom.

"Take the hemorrhoid commercial. You can sustain your-self, make a good living off commercials playing to nostalgia."

"I don't need the money. I need..."

"Liam. Buddy. You know what they call you around town?"

I shake my head. I don't want to know, but I can't get an objection past the lump in my throat.

"Has-been Stone. Super zero. Crazy Comic Coo-Coo Nut."

"Alright," I say. I don't need to hear more. But he continues.

"There's a joke that's been going around. Knock, knock."

I guess this is the part where I hear how complete and total my fall from Hollywood grace is.

"Who's there?" I ask. My shoulders bunch, waiting for the blow.

"Liam Stone," Devon says.

"Liam Stone who?"

He looks me square in the eye and says, "Exactly."

Devon lets the meaning of the joke sink in. Liam Stone who? Exactly.

I've been forgotten. I'm a has-been.

"There's nothing I can do?" I ask.

"Buddy. You trashed a movie set. You lost your shit, had some crazy breakdown, and now your name is mud. I can't fix crazy."

"I'm not..." I stop.

I see myself through his eyes. The world's eyes. I look like hell. I live as a hermit. I'm not to be trusted. My shoulders fall. There's a heavy weight on me that has nothing to do with the calendar date.

"I'll get back to you about the commercial," I say.

"That's my boy," Devon says. And without a goodbye he hangs up.

I hold the phone, stare at my face still pictured in the camera.

Once, it graced movie screens around the world. Once, it was loved by millions.

Now...

I was like a light bulb. Hollywood plugged me in and while I shone brightly they made millions. But as soon as I dimmed, they took me down, and threw me out. Within five seconds, they had another lightbulb, shining just as brightly as me. I was replaceable. I didn't realize it while I was shining. But to Hollywood, actors aren't people, they're commodities.

I was a commodity.

But even knowing that, I'd still give anything to go back. To shine again. To be loved by millions.

3

Ginny

"Would you pass the potatoes please?" asks Heather.

"Sure," I say. I lift the antique dish piled with mashed potatoes. Enid always pulls out the heirloom china when Heather and her husband come for Sunday dinner. I hand Heather the dish and she wrinkles her nose.

"How are things?" she asks.

"Good," I say. I learned years ago that the less said around Heather the better.

Her husband, Mayor Joel Wilson, chuckles and stretches back in his chair. "That's good. Real good. I was worried we'd have to find you a job somewhere."

I smile, which probably looks more like a wolverine gritting its teeth. I'm still working as a personal trainer and fitness instructor, the same job I've been at for the past three years. As Joel knows.

"Can't have welfare cases in the family," Joel says to the rest of the table.

"She's not family," says Finick. He's Heather's much younger brother, and her ward since their parents passed last year.

"Thankfully," says Redge, Heather's son. "Wilsons aren't losers." He's a little older than Bean. He has the bullet-shaped head of his dad and the personality of his mom.

"We went to see Liam Stone," says Bean. She bounces in her seat and a few peas roll off her plate.

"Tsk, Beatrice," says Enid. "Don't interrupt."

"Sorry, Grandma. But can you believe it? We went to Liam Stone's headquarters. It was so cool, and we're going to go back soon, and he'll train me to be a superhero and I can't wait."

Enid cuts me a sharp look. I didn't meet her until after George died. George and I married a month after we met, and he died two weeks later. I met his family, including his mom Enid, at the funeral home.

When she saw me for the first time, she looked me over, and said, *'I wish he'd let you die.'*

I agreed with her. George and I were fighting, some stupid early marriage spat that didn't mean anything. He was driving and I yelled something and he missed a curve in the road. We rolled, went into the water and...I couldn't get out. He'd swum to the surface. He'd made it out. But my seatbelt wouldn't come loose. I clawed at it. I fought. I was frantic. I knew I was going to die. It was done.

Drowning, it's the scariest thing in the world, the most terrifying...until you stop struggling. Then, it's almost pleasant. That's what terrifies me, going back to that time, and remembering the moment where it was peaceful, where nothing scared me anymore, and whether I lived or died didn't matter.

But George came back. Before I lost consciousness I saw him. The light from the surface surrounded him, he swam to me, his arms pushed through the water, he was so vital, so determined and alive. Then, I ran out of air. I lost sight of him, I lost...

I woke up in the hospital. And he was gone.

He didn't make it. Going back in for me, going back, something happened, he was cut, he was hurt, he bled out. He bled out on the grass while I was unconscious next to him. And, what...what could I say to his mother, the woman I'd never met who blamed me for his death? What could I say? Nothing, except *me too*. I wished that too. Until I realized I was pregnant with Bean and then I knew that I had to live and do everything I could to protect her and keep her safe and happy and alive. For him.

But.

I've failed at that too. And my promise to George to always take care of Bean, to keep her safe. I can't keep it, because life had other plans. Didn't it?

I stick my fork into the pot roast on my plate and saw at it with my knife. Slowly I tune back into the conversation. Bean's telling them about Liam Stone's trailer and her theory that there's a top secret base underneath the rusted out single-wide.

Grandma Enid sends a pointed glare my way. She doesn't approve of Bean's superhero obsession. At all.

Grandpa Clark sits at the head of the table. He flips through a magazine for World War II models. Heather whispers something in Joel's ear and he grunts his approval. Redge makes food art with his mash potatoes and peas. And Finick plays a handheld video game in his lap under the table. Nobody's paying attention.

Except... "This is not an appropriate activity for Beatrice," hisses Enid. "Stop filling her head with this trash."

"It's not trash," says Finick. He drops his game on the table. He's grown nearly four inches in the past few months and his voice has deepened. He uses the new depth to inject scorn into the statement. "If Bean wants to be a superhero, let her."

"Superheroes aren't real," says Enid.

Bean gasps.

"They're not. Only babies think they are," says Redge. He sticks his tongue out at Bean. "Mom was going to get Liam Stone for my birthday party, but she says he's a drunk now and not fit to be around decent people."

Bean hits her hands on the table and springs up. "Take it back."

"No way," says Redge. "Superheroes aren't real."

"Shut it, you little troglodyte," says Finick.

"Apologize, Fin, right now," says Heather.

"No. You aren't my mom."

Heather's lips pinch and I catch a vein pulsing in her temple.

"Come here, Bean," I whisper. I motion for her to climb in my lap. I wrap my arms around her and snuggle her close. "Don't worry about it, baby," I say. "Heroes are real." I kiss her on her head.

"Course they are," says Finick. He shoots a glare at Heather. "Anybody can be a hero. You just have to be willing to do something selfless."

Grandma Enid drops her silverware and pushes her plate away. "The only thing selflessness does, Finick O'Connor, is get you dead."

All the noise at the table stops. Everyone stares at Enid's tight face and the deep lines around her permanently pinched lips.

Then Grandpa Clark jerks his chair back. It scrapes loudly against the wood floor. "That's enough," he says in a loud voice. He takes a deep breath of air and looks around at Mayor Wilson's shocked face. Heather's distaste. Redge's gloating sneer. Finick's defiance. Bean in my lap. And his wife Enid and her tight, pursed mouth.

"That's enough"—he clears his throat—"pot roast for a good while. Anyone for pie? Enid made pecan."

He walks from the dining room to the kitchen. The door swings shut after him.

"Is Grandpa Clark alright?" asks Bean.

I rub my knuckles against her head. "Course he is. Right as rain."

"He just wants you to be a princess, not a superhero," says Enid. But there's no fire in her voice, only a hollow fatigue.

"Don't want to be a princess, Grandma."

"How about you kids go in to the living room and watch some cartoons," says Enid. "We'll bring pie in a few minutes."

Bean slips off my lap, and she, Redge, and Finick head to couch. The house is small, it's a single-story Cape Cod, built in the 1950s. It has two bedrooms, a kitchen, a living room, and one bathroom. The carpet is avocado green, the walls are wood-paneled, and every surface is cluttered with Grandpa Clark's military battle model kits and Grandma Enid's porcelain figurines. Sometimes I try to imagine George growing up here, but I can't. There's not much of him in the clutter. His childhood bedroom has long since been converted into Grandpa Clark's miniature model building workshop and Grandma Enid gave all of George's possessions to charity. There's nothing here of him.

It used to make me sad, but now it's just how it is. I grew up out west and never saw the house looking different anyway.

Bean and I live in the garage. It was a two stall. Grandpa Clark converted it to a studio apartment when Bean was diagnosed and I realized my salary didn't cover all Bean's medical expenses, as well as a place to live. Not to mention food, childcare, car insurance, gas, utilities, clothing, phone bills, the list goes on. I didn't have the money. Enid and Clark were kind enough to offer us a place to live. I can never thank them enough. Without their support...I don't know how I would've survived.

Heather clears her throat and turns to me. "Seriously, Genevieve. I want to warn you. I knew Liam Stone when we acted together." She rubs her blonde hair between her fingers and smiles. She likes to mention all the actors she's run across. "He was a bad apple before, and he's a rotten apple now."

"More like pickled," says Joel, and he laughs.

Enid sniffs. "I wish you wouldn't get Beatrice's hopes up. False hope does more damage than no hope."

I take the cloth napkin out of my lap and set it on the table. The starched fabric scratches against my fingers. "Thanks for your concern," I say.

"Hardheaded," mutters Enid.

Heather reaches over and pats her arm. Enid sends her a warm smile. I wait for Enid to tell Heather that *she's the daughter of her heart,*" but she doesn't say anything. It's no secret in town that Heather and George dated for five years, and had only been broken up for a few weeks before I entered the picture. Enid had dreamed for years of Heather becoming her daughter-in-law. They're two peas in a pod. I'm not from here though, so I didn't know. In the short time I knew him, George never mentioned he had a hopeful bride back in Southern Ohio. Since George's death, Enid and Heather have remained as close as mother and daughter. Sunday dinners, birthdays, holidays...even though George and Heather didn't marry, she's a fixture in his parents' life. She's the daughter of Enid's heart. And now Joel is Enid's adopted son-in-law, Finick and Redge her adopted grandchildren.

"How's that boy?" asks Enid. We all know she's talking about Finick. She always refers to him as *that boy.*

"Joel caught him sneaking out again. He's leaving at midnight, not coming home until four in the morning."

"Terrible," says Enid.

"He's running with the wrong crowd," says Joel. "Next time I get a phone call from the police, I won't be talking him out of trouble."

Enid tsks, "Poor boy." Then she turns back to me, "You need to stay away from that Liam Stone. He'll bring nothing but misery."

"The only thing he cares about is drink," says Heather.

Clark brings out the pie, and everyone forgets conversation. It's bourbon pecan, and the bourbon bites my tongue.

What do I do? What do I do?

I hear Bean laughing. It's a good day today, she's up and moving, laughing and interacting. But not every day is good, and soon there might not be any days at all.

Not one.

I poke at the pie, and the bourbon wafts up again.

What had Liam Stone said? Don't come back unless you're bringing Lagavulin?

"Is Lagavulin liquor?" I ask.

Joel guffaws. "That's a fine Scotch, that. You don't put it in *pie*."

Everyone goes back to their conversation, but my mind seizes onto an idea. I think about it, then decide, yes, it just might work. I'll go back. Alone this time. And give Liam Stone *exactly* what he asked for.

4

Liam

The questions plagued me for a long, sleepless night. What am I going to do? Where to from here? Where do you go after you've hit bottom?

When the guy-wire snapped and I fell, I experienced the worst terror of my life. My mind was so wrapped in fear that my body shut down. I couldn't yell, I couldn't struggle, there was nothing I could do except anticipate my bones shattering as I hit the concrete. And they did. I can still hear the exact crunching noise in my mind when my back broke, and my hip bone crumbled, like a ball of chalk slamming into pavement and crumbling to dust.

It took a long time to come out of that place, where I was lying on the concrete and there was only my breath and the pain. But I did. I did what everyone expected. Had the surgeries, the physical therapy, took the pain medication, did it all. And went back to being Liam Stone, just with a fake hip and a pieced together spine. The only thing I didn't anticipate was what would happen when I got strapped back into the harness and hung suspended in the air.

Hell happened.

And I was back again, falling, and not able to do anything but...

Well, ask the world, there are plenty of videos of me out there, "losing my shit" on set.

That was two years ago.

But yesterday was the first day anyone's actually said *"it's over."*

Although, I knew. Why else would I be hiding out in the rural Midwest, living as a hermit? I have to face the facts. I got asked to be a clown, for crying out loud. A clown. And a celebrity pusher of hemorrhoid cures.

When night came, it was dark and lonely. I cleaned up the trailer, threw out a dozen beer bottles, swept up months of dirt, washed the sheets, took a shower, shaved, found clean clothes. All the while I thought, and thought.

After twelve hours of insomniac pacing I decided that the only place I can go is up. I've had two years to sink to this level. Look at me, for crying out loud. But now that I'm here, I can kick off the bottom and use the momentum to swim even higher than before. That's the benefit of hitting bottom, if it doesn't kill you, you can spring back up. That's what I'll do.

I'm going to get fit, get my head straight, beat my fear, I'm going to do something heroic, something great that will make the world love me again. Because if I don't, I'll spend the rest of my life pimping out to birthday parties and adult diaper commercials. And that future is scarier than facing the harness and the guy-wire again.

I lie down in the hammock outside in the shade and close my eyes. Now that I've come to a decision I'm ready to sleep. It seems like I just closed my eyes when cold liquid splashes over my face.

"Get up," a sharp voice snaps. "Get up. Don't you have any pride left? Get up."

I gasp and shoot straight up. My arms wave and I try to catch myself, but the hammock spins and I fall to the dirt.

"Jeez Louise," a woman says.

I shake my head and fling the drops of liquid off my face. I'm on all fours in the dirt. I take a moment to draw in a deep breath. That's whiskey I smell. I wipe my face. The coarse dirt mixes with the sticky liquor and sticks to my skin. My T-shirt is soaked through and my hair's dripping. I shake off again, then, "What's wrong with you?" I stand up and turn to the woman.

"You," I say. Because it's that short, pushy brunette from yesterday morning.

"Me," she says. Then she holds up a bottle of bottom-shelf whiskey. "They didn't have any Lagavulin so I brought you this instead."

"Are you insane?" I ask. I wipe at my face again, but it only rubs the dirt and liquor around even more.

"You said I shouldn't come back unless I brought your Lagavulin. Well, sorry, mister, but they don't have fancy schmancy drink in Centreville. So I brought you second best."

"More like hundredth best," I say. I turn from her so that she doesn't see the smile aching to rise up at the corner of my mouth.

I'm starting to get my bearings now that the groggy confusion of being woken up by whiskey has passed. "You were here yesterday," I say.

"That's right," she says. "I have something important to ask. But you seemed to be..."—she pauses and considers her words —"indisposed."

"Well." I climb back into the hammock and close my eyes. "Consider me indisposed for the rest of forever."

She makes a little angry sound under her breath and my ears perk up like they like what they hear.

"Sorry I dunked you in liquor. I lost my temper...I got a bad call this morning. About..."

My ears twitch. It's funny, I haven't had company in years, and now I sort of don't want her to go away. She has a low voice, sweet and husky at the same time. It sort of strums over me and makes me want to hear more. It mixes with the scent of the whiskey on my skin and makes me feel drunk with the sound of her.

My body tenses, waiting for more of her strumming voice to roll over me. But she stays quiet. I guess she's going to leave. Too bad.

"You going already?" I ask. I don't open my eyes to check. It sort of seems like it would be hard to watch her walk away.

But then, she lets out another angry noise. Suddenly, she shoves at the hammock. Hard. It tilts and I'm dumped to the ground. I hit with a thud, and pain shoots through my back. I tense and clutch the grass until the pain subsides.

"Dang it all, woman. Are you insane?"

I roll over and lay there, waiting for the pain to completely clear.

She stands over me, her hands on her hips. How doesn't she have any fear? I'm an unknown man, a crazy drunk as far as she's concerned, and she's here like some avenging angel, no fear whatsoever. I know movies, and the only time someone acts like that is when they've got nothing to lose. She's not crazy. I squint and look at her eyes.

No. She's not crazy. She's desperate.

I let out a long sigh and rub my hand down my face.

"Sorry," she says again. But I don't think she is. I stare up at the leaves of the oak trees, and the light filtering through. She's backlit like a superhero on a cover, and I'm the chump she's toppled. "I need to talk with you," she says.

"Gathered that," I say. I keep progressively relaxing the muscles in my back to stop the spasms. "Give me a second."

She nods and then leans against the trunk of the big oak tree. I feel her eyes on me as I finish the sequence. It's been a long time since I've felt the heat of a woman's gaze, and while my back is relaxing, another part of me gets a lot tenser.

I try to quell the reaction, but it's a losing battle. The second she started talking my body started reacting. Except, maybe it's more than that, because she's quiet now and I'm still feeling her effect. Finally, I'm able to sit up. I scoot back and lean against the tree. The trunk is thick and wide enough for the both of us to relax against. I pat the grass next to me.

"Have a seat," I say.

She hesitates, then slowly sits down as far from me as possible while still leaning against the bark.

"What can I do you for?" I ask, opting to ditch the Hollywood and go for good ol' boy.

She clears her throat. "Right..." She stops, folds her hands, looks away.

It's funny, now that the whiskey dumping and the hammock dumping are done, she seems almost shy.

"You want something? Tell me it's not a birthday party request," I say, trying to lighten the mood. "I don't do balloon animals."

She lets out a little huff, an almost laugh, and then looks at me. I'm struck by the freckles sprinkled across her nose and cheeks. The carefree and youthful feature seems so out of place on a woman with such a serious demeanor.

"I came looking for help," she says. Studying her face, I'd never know that she was anything but calm and determined. But I'm an actor, and I look beyond expressions. I watch her hands. They twist in her lap, and she clasps them together to try and keep in the emotion. Nerves. Worry. Fear.

I should tell her to go away. To not bother me again. I've got enough troubles of my own without letting her dump whatever's wrong in her life on me. I'm not a fixer. But...there's something about her, about the way she looks at me. Not like I'm a has-been, but like I'm a *could-be*.

"Alright," I say. "I'm listening."

She closes her eyes and her shoulders fall an inch. "My daughter," she says. "You're her hero. I mean, Liam Stone is."

She opens her eyes and turns to me. I nod to show my understanding. My character has the same name as I do, it was an executive decision to make me a *brand*.

"She wants to be a superhero too. The only way she knows how is to train under a real superhero. Just like in the comic books. And you're the only superhero in the world. I want...I mean...I'm asking if you would train my daughter."

I lean away from the woman. So, I was wrong, she's not desperate, she actually is insane. A crazed fan. I saw enough of them in the past. They can't tell the difference between me and the character I play. It's resulted in some bad scenes in the past.

I'm disappointed. I didn't realize how much I wanted her to be something *more*, until I realized she wasn't.

"Sure thing," I say in a voice that I hope is impersonal. "I'll get you an autograph. Sign some comics for you." I go to stand up, let the woman leave with some memorabilia.

"No," she says. She grabs my arm. "Please."

I look down at her hand. She blushes and pulls back.

"I'm sorry. You just...you don't understand."

"Okay," I say. But I think I do. "What's your name?"

"Ginny," she says. "Ginny Weaver."

"Alright, Ginny Weaver. I'm Liam Stone. But I'm not a superhero. I'm an actor. I played a superhero. You understand? It's pretend." You have to be careful when explaining these things. Sometimes, it gets a little hairy.

She squeezes her eyes shut and shakes her head. Then, "I know that. I'm asking for my daughter. She's sick."

On the word "sick," her voice catches. And I realize that I misread the situation.

Ginny looks at me and I nod my understanding. "Go on."

"I got a call this morning."

"You said that."

"The doctors." She wipes at her eyes, even though I don't see any tears. "Sorry. I'm sorry. I haven't told anyone yet."

I wait until she pushes down whatever she's wrestling with.

"The leukemia went into remission, then it came back almost right away. It's a really rare type. Aggressive. It's not getting better. Bean, my daughter, she needs a bone marrow donor. They told me it's her best chance."

I see a little white clover flower and I pluck it. I need to keep my hands busy, I can't sit still while she tells me about this little girl. I pull another flower head up and drop it next to the first.

"They called this morning," she whispers. "Still nothing. No matching donors, not in any of the registries. Not anywhere. And soon, she'll be too sick for a transplant anyway."

I drop a third flower head. "What does that mean?" I ask.

"It means...don't make me say it."

I nod. I don't know this woman, I don't know anything about her except she's kind of crazy and she loves her daughter. But, even with that, I move closer and put my hand on her arm. At my touch she takes in a shaky breath and a small sound escapes her lips.

"She has a letter for you," she says. She uses her forearm to brush at her eyes, then she pulls an envelope from her pocket. "I don't know what it says. She's barely six years old, but she's precocious."

I nod and take the folded envelope. I break open the letter and pull out a blue piece of construction paper. There's a picture of me, in my Liam Stone outfit, black leather and a cape. And there's a girl next to me in a cape and mask, it says *Bean* beneath her.

I glance over at Ginny. Her face is turned away. She's giving me space to read, or she's giving herself space to collect herself.

I read Bean's letter. It's written in crayon. Not all the words are spelled correctly and some of the B's and P's are backwards.

*D*ear Liam Stone,
     Everyone says you aren't real. Except my mom. She believes in you, and so do I.
     I want to learn to be a superhero. My dad was a hero. He died saving my mama and me. I want to be a hero too. Like my dad and you. Will you teach me?
     Bean

I hold the letter and stare at the words until they blur. My hand shakes and so I take the letter, carefully fold it, and put it in my pocket.

I can't...I'm not what this girl needs. I'm not really a hero. I'm just an actor, a messed up, has-been actor, with a broken body and a bad reputation. I only just decided that I'm going to climb myself out of this hole I'm in. I can't carry a woman and her sick daughter up with me too.

"I'm not..." I pause when Ginny jerks in surprise and wipes at her eyes. Her back's turned to me. After a minute she turns back to me. Her eyes are red, but she's composed.

"What?" she says.

I drop my eyes, see the clover heads and swipe them away. "I'm not one of those charities that grants wishes," I say. The words feel dirty in my mouth. But I'm not, I'm not the right person for this.

Ginny's face is calm, but her hands clench. "You're saying no?"

I swallow down the flavor of shame. "I'm saying no."

I can't help them. I've got nothing to give.

"Please," she says. She drops her eyes. "I'll do anything."

30

I see it in her eyes. She will. Anything I ask, this woman will do it. I feel sick with the shame of it. "I'm not asking," I say, suddenly angry. "I'm not a hero. I'm not the person you need. Have you looked at me? What can I give her?"

She flinches then takes in my appearance. The still-damp T-shirt, my dirt-covered hands and face. My out-of-shape body and pain-worn face. Finally, Ginny nods. She understands, I can see it.

"Are you an alcoholic?" she asks. Her voice is calm and matter-of-fact.

"No. Yesterday was a once-a-year anomaly. I don't drink."

"Drugs?"

"No."

"Just self-pity then," she says.

I let out a harsh laugh. I'm on to her brand of crazy and I'm starting to like it. She's quick with the punches and she doesn't hold back. Honest and direct.

She considers me for a moment, then, "I'll train you," she says. She leans toward me and nods. "It's perfect. I'll train you."

"What do you mean?" I ask. My eyes are drawn to the top of her breasts, suddenly visible in the dip of her tank top.

"I'm a fitness instructor. I'm taking classes in sports medicine. I can train you, get you in the best shape of your life. You can work with Bean. And I'll train you. A sort of superhero academy. Everyone will come out on top. Everyone will win." She stops, swallows whatever she was going to say that has a shadow passing over her face. "When you're done here. When Bean's...you can go back to Hollywood. You'll be in top form."

I poke at the little ball of hope that forms in my chest. Is it real? Can I trust it? I didn't like the feeling I got when she mentioned what would happen after her daughter, well, died. Can I really do this? Get involved?

Except, this does seem like the answer I'm seeking. The day I decide I'm going to get my act together, Ginny shows and offers to train me. And if I help them, maybe the world will see me as a hero again.

Maybe the studio execs would scramble to hire me again rather than toss me to the bottom level of actor hell.

I can't quell the fierce need that arises at the thought. I could be on top of the world again. I will be.

"Deal," I say.

"Really?" Ginny's voice is high and surprised.

I give a wry smile and hold out my hand. "It's a deal. I'll train your daughter to be a superhero. You train me."

We shake and our bargain is sealed.

5

Ginny

"It doesn't fit," says Liam. His looks down at himself in disgust.

The spandex of his black pants stretches tight, and his shirt rides up over his gut.

"Huh." I look him over. He's right, it's about two sizes too small.

He stretches his legs and arms. The fabric pulls and he winces. We're in his living room, it's been cleaned up since I saw it from the door yesterday. Liam's showered and dressed in his alter ego's costume.

It doesn't look great. In fact, he looks like a low-budget imitation of himself. Put him next to a movie poster and he's the paler, older, softer version of Liam Stone. Although, also, maybe a little more approachable, as the Greek god look meant mere mortals couldn't approach him. And we can get it straight right now, I'm just a mere mortal.

Oh well.

Liam swings his arms and then shakes his head as the shirt rides higher.

"It fits good enough," I say.

He sighs and pulls down the shirt. "There's no reason to wear it."

Okay, I get it. He's embarrassed. The last time he wore this outfit he looked like an Olympic athlete. Now, not so much. But who's judging? It's not like he needs to impress me with his looks. I couldn't give a rat's ass about his looks. I care about him being *nice*. To my daughter.

"There's every reason," I say. "You aren't *Liam Stone* unless you're wearing the costume. You can't train Bean unless you're *him*."

"I could train your daughter in normal clothes. I wore normal clothes in my films."

But when he was being *heroic*, he wore his costume.

"No deal," I say.

He grits his teeth and gestures to himself. "It's embarrassing."

I look around the trailer. The lighting's dim, but I've had enough time to take it in. There isn't anything personal here. Nothing to remind him of his past. It's just a ratty couch, an old wooden kitchen table, a folding chair, and a tv on the floor. That's it. No pictures, no knick-knacks, no magazines or books, nothing. I'm surprised he had this costume, although he did have to pull it out of a cardboard box from the back of his bedroom closet. But there's nothing here to connect him to his past, and nothing here to hold him to the present either. He stopped living.

I've been there. It looked different when it happened to me but I recognize it.

I step forward. "Let's get this straight," I say.

He narrows his eyes. "What?"

I move closer, touch the fabric of the cape draped over his shoulders.

"I don't give a crap what you look like."

"What?"

"I don't give a crap if you are dripping sex appeal, or if you look like an orangutan's butt."

"Jeez." He gives me an incredulous look, but I keep going.

"None of that matters. What you look like doesn't matter. It's what you do that matters."

He shakes his head. Either he thinks I'm crazy or he's doesn't believe me.

"Repeat after me. Even if I look like an orangutan..."

"Are you kidding?"

I poke him in his spandex-clad chest. "No. Repeat."

He sighs, "Even if I look like an orangutan."

"It doesn't matter."

"It doesn't matter," he says.

"Because I'm effin' Liam Stone."

He chokes on a laugh.

"Say it," I say.

A wry smile curves his lip.

"Because I'm effin' Liam Stone."

"And the world is my bitch."

He starts laughing. It starts as a small chuckle, then it gets louder.

"Say it."

"The world is my bitch."

He grins and I catch my breath. He looks more handsome, more gorgeous than I've ever seen him. On screen, he was sexy, but here and now, he's...wow, if the world could see him now. That's why he was famous, not for his talent, but for this raw magnetism.

I curl my fingers and fight the urge to touch him.

I clear my throat. "You're effin' Liam Stone," I say. "Now act like it."

He fights the smile on his face, tries to put it away but can't. "You're crazy, you know?"

"Yeah. I know." I smile back.

He looks at me, and his eyes turn warm and happy. There's a ripple low in my belly that responds to his look. I've not felt anything like that in nearly seven years. I stand in the thick silence and take in the feel of his eyes stroking over me. For a moment, I'm just a woman and he's just a man. My lips part and my breath catches. There's nothing there, not his ruined career, not my being a widow, or trying to get Bean...

Bean.

I clear my throat and break eye contact.

"Hey," he says. He reaches for me and I step back.

"You ready?" I ask. I blush at the low, throaty sound of my voice. Years ago I was told my voice makes a man think of sex and cigarettes. This is the first time I've been able to hear it myself.

"Sure," he says. He drops his hand and I relax. "Thanks for that."

"Of course." I clear my throat again. Then, "Come on. You can ride with me."

"We're doing this?"

I nod. "Training starts today."

6

Liam

$\mathcal{W}$e roll up to a tiny yellow Cape Cod with brown shutters. Ginny steers her beater into a grassy parking area next to the garage. Her stereo blasts bass heavy pop and as I step out of the car, my cape blows in the wind. A boy rides by on his bike, and as he passes he turns his head to stare.

"I'm effin' Liam Stone," I say under my breath, because right now I feel like this is the stupidest decision I've ever made and I need some bolstering.

I shut my door and plant my feet on the dry grass. Then I take a look around. The street's packed tight with small houses. They vary on a theme. Small, yellow, beige, or white, chain-link fences and brown grass. Some have flowers, most don't. Some have boarded windows, most don't. There's a house on the end with a rusted car on concrete blocks.

Ginny cuts the engine, the music stops, and she steps out of the car.

"Welcome to Centreville," she says.

I swipe at my cape. The flipping thing is blowing around like we're on a movie set and I'm posing for the movie poster shot.

I follow her as she walks through the grass to the front door. I'm a good ten feet behind Ginny, she's moving fast. Before we reach it, the door opens and a little girl rushes out. She's bald and wearing pair of shorts and a striped shirt with a cape. I'd bet my last dollar this is Bean.

She only has eyes for her mom. She runs up and hurls herself into Ginny's arms.

"Mama. You're back. Finick and Redge are here. Miss Heather dropped them off for Gran to watch. Miss Heather's going to the salon. They don't allow kids, 'cause it's fancy, but she said boys don't go to salons and a girl like me don't need one 'cause I don't have hair anymore, and then Finick said '*stuff it*' and a bad word, then Heather said '*watch your mouth*,' and Finick said '*you ain't my mom*,' and then—"

I stare at the kid in amazement. She hasn't taken a breath. In fact, the whole story has been one long word with no pauses. She hasn't noticed me yet, either. It's incredible. Ginny squats down and nods her head as she listens to her daughter.

Bean gulps a big breath.

"Where's Grandma?" Ginny asks.

Bean pauses. "At the store, 'cause we were out of pickles and she said pickles are the only thing that stop hot flashes and misery. Then Finick said that there's other things, and Gran said—"

"Where's Finick?"

"He's in the basement playing video games. But Grandpa said he shouldn't because playing video games makes kids crazy and then—"

"Where's Grandpa?"

"He's looking for the ladder." Bean doesn't say anything

else. Instead she makes her eyes real big and purses her lips like she's trying not to say anymore.

"Why's he looking for the ladder?"

Bean's folds her lips until they're a thin line.

"Bean?"

Her face turns red and then she lets out a long exasperated breath. "'Cause."

"Yeah?"

"'Cause I whooped Redge at Chinese checkers so he threw my Liam Stone action figure in the highest branch of the walnut tree, then I cried and he called me a big baby, then Grandpa came out and said he'd have to find the ladder."

She sighs and wraps her arms around herself.

Ginny pulls her closer and kisses her head. "Don't worry. I've got something better than an action figure."

Bean sniffs.

Then I step into her line of sight. Her eyes go wide, they travel up me from my feet all the way to my face. Then she does something I don't expect. She lets out a scream and starts jumping up and down.

Ginny turns to me and grins.

Finally, Bean throws another hug around her mom. "He's here, he's here."

Ginny laughs and I'm stunned at the joy I hear in it.

Bean looks up at me, awe on her face. "I knew you were real. Redge said you aren't real, but I knew you were."

My cape flutters and now I'm grateful for the wind. I feel like I can't let this kid down.

"That's right. I'm real," I say. "I'm Liam Stone."

"You know what that means?" asks Bean.

"What's that?"

"Grandpa doesn't need a ladder. You can fly up and get my action figure."

~

*T*he tree is a big old walnut tree, about thirty feet high. The action figure, a terrible replica of me, with a black cape and an S on the shirt, hangs from a branch about three quarters of the way to the top. Twenty feet up. Sure. I can do this.

"You don't have to do this," whispers Ginny.

She's pulled me aside. She actually looks concerned for me, which makes me worry what my face looks like. Bean, the little bully Redge, Bean's grandpa, and an angsty-looking teen named Finick are all here. The grandma is back from the store and in the kitchen making pickles and lemonade for "the show."

"It's fine," I say. I wipe at a line of sweet running down my face.

Granted, when I saw the height of the tree I wanted to turn around and run. I never climbed trees as a kid. And whenever I climbed in the movies, I was strapped in a safety harness. But even the harness didn't keep me from falling.

I blow out a long breath.

"Gotta do it sometime," I say.

"Yeah. But this isn't part of the training. I was going to have you run. Lift weights. Not...are you gonna be sick?"

"I'm fine."

I walk to the trunk of the tree. The lowest branch is about five feet off the ground. If I grab it I can swing myself up.

"Five bucks he doesn't get it," says Redge.

"Of course he'll get it," says Bean. "He's a superhero."

"Then why hasn't he flown?"

"Because he wants to climb," says Bean.

"No, it's because he's a loser."

"Watch it," says Finick, in a warning tone.

"Children," says the grandpa.

"I don't have to *watch it*, my dad's the mayor. And that guy in the cape. He's just a loser," says Redge.

Bean gasps.

I don't turn to look. I can feel them watching. Bean's hopeful gaze. Redge's sneer. Finick's teenage disdain. I can even feel Ginny's gaze. A woman who has clearly seen it all is looking at me with something like...belief.

I grab the rough bark and grunt as I hoist myself up onto the first limb.

"Yeah," shouts Bean.

Redge makes a rude noise.

I test the strength of the limb and then slowly stand. I grab the branch a few feet above me and yank myself up again.

I keep climbing. After the fifth limb my arms start to burn from dragging my weight up. I'm only one more limb away from reaching the action figure when I make the mistake of looking down.

My head spins and the panic rushes at me. It's so fast that I can't stop it. My heart pounds, my throat closes and I can't breathe. My vision starts to go dark and I'm going to fall, I'm going to fall, I'm...I sway, start to lose my grip. I cry out. I drop my body to the limb and wrap my arms and legs around it.

My breath comes out in hard pants. Hell. Hell.

I close my eyes. My heart pounds and I'm wrapped around a tree limb nearly thirty feet in the air.

The wind gusts a little stronger than before and the limb I'm plastered to creaks and sways.

I don't have control anymore. I can't seem to open my eyes. I can't let go of the branch. I can't get up.

"Liam?" It's Ginny. She's calling up to me. "Liam? Are you okay?"

I can't answer. My throat is so narrow, my body so much in the grip of fear that I can't open my mouth to respond.

"You all right up there?" she calls.

"What a loser," says Redge.

"He is *not*," says Bean.

"Is so. Look at him. He's like a baby. Rock a bye baby in a tree top."

"Liam?" shouts Ginny. "Are you all right?"

I pry my eyes open. Keep them open even when the world tilts and my heart picks up speed again.

I can do this. I'm effin' Liam Stone. The words don't help. I try it again. I'm effin' Liam Stone.

"I'm coming up," shouts Ginny.

There's some argument down below. Something about calling the fire department. I tune them out. I can do this. I can get past this.

Slowly, I crawl up and wrap my arms around the limb above me. It shakes in my hands. I stretch up and reach as far as I can and there...just, there. I extend my fingers until finally I grab the cape of the action figure.

"Got it!"

Yes.

A loud cheer comes from below. Now I just have to get down. And finally, I have sympathy for all those cats that can climb up a tree but need the friendly fireman to pull them down.

I let out a long breath.

"Come on, loser."

"Quiet, Redge," says Ginny.

She trots over to the tree and pulls herself up into the lowest branch. "You need help up there?" she calls through the leaves.

I could say yes. They could call the fire department and bring me down with the ladder. If I do that, I can kiss all this goodbye. I can go back to my trailer, to never playing a movie role again. Or I can climb down on my own and pursue this, try to win my life back. It's not an abstract idea anymore. The choice is right in front of me.

The wind blows and the tree shudders again. I shudder with it. But... "I got this."

"Yeah?"

"Yeah."

Thirty excruciating minutes later I make it to the ground.

The only people left in the back yard are Ginny and Bean. Redge, Finick, Grandpa and the pickle grandma all got tired of watching after ten minutes of me hugging one limb.

I hand the action figure to Bean.

"You did it," she says. Her eyes glow and she hugs the figure to her chest.

"Sure did."

"I knew you would."

I wink at her. That makes one of us.

7

Liam

"Ten more. Grit your teeth and pull," says Ginny.

I pull up on the makeshift pullup bar attached to the oak tree in my front yard. My muscles burn and sweat runs down my face. Not even the best trainers in Los Angeles can compare to the superhero boot camp hell that Ginny's prepared.

"Nine," she says when my chin finally clears the bar.

I slowly lower my body, careful not to let my feet touch the ground.

"Keep your knees up."

I grunt. I don't have energy for a response.

"Eight."

Sweat drips into my eyes. I concentrate on finishing the reps. And soon I'm done with the final ten. I drop to the ground and shake out my arms and roll my shoulders.

"That was good," she says.

I stretch my arms. It's not even six a.m. and I think I've done more exercise today than I have in the past two years.

"Did you ever think about being a drill sergeant?" I ask.

"Har har," says Ginny.

It's warm in August in southern Ohio, even before the sun comes up. Ginny's wearing tight little shorts and an open-backed tank top. And I think that I might be hot for gym teacher. Even as tough as it is, I'm enjoying every bit of her ordering me around.

She has a clipboard with every exercise and rep written out. She means business.

"All done?" I ask.

She snorts. "Are you kidding? It's only been an hour. I've given myself a month to get you in top shape. You need to be working out at least six hours per day. Two hours this morning and I'm leaving you a schedule for this afternoon and evening. Rest time's up, give me twenty-five military push-ups."

And on it goes. When I don't know an exercise, Ginny gets down and does it right next to me. Diamond pushups, incline pushups, pullups...we're working on shoulders and arms this morning.

Tomorrow is legs, the schedule is full of squats, lunges, and other versions of hell meant to make me feel like my legs are made of Jell-O. The day after is back and abs and some sort of warped yoga that Ginny claims will burn more than all the weight lifting exercises combined.

"Keep it up," says Ginny.

I finish out the push-ups and grin. As hot and tired as I am, I feel invigorated.

"How's your back? And your hip?" asks Ginny. She's modi-fied the exercises so that they strengthen and protect rather than harm.

"I'm good," I say.

"Here." Ginny tosses a water bottle to me. I take a drink of the ice water and hand it back when I'm done. I walk next to her as we head to the large tire that she brought so I can lug it around the yard.

I start the exercise.

"I was thinking," she says.

I keep tugging. "Yeah?"

"Yesterday, in the tree...that wasn't because you were out of shape."

I shove the tire up and flip it back to the ground. It's hard to say out loud, hard to admit. "No," I say.

I keep at the tire and wait for her to ask more questions. I'm sure she's seen the videos of me trashing the movie sets. Her and a hundred million other people. Maybe she's connecting the dots. When I get too high, when I'm reminded of the fall, I...lose it. But after a whole twenty yards of shoving and flipping the tire she still hasn't said anything. I let the tire hit the ground and dirt flies up in a cloud at the impact.

"That it?" I ask.

She nods. Then she walks back to the tree and starts a cool-down sequence. I follow her motions. Stretch the legs, the arms, the back. I start to relax and my muscles unwind. I watch Ginny for the next move. She crosses one leg over the other and bends down. I swallow. She's got the pertest, most nicely formed behind I've seen in...ever. I was exhausted, now I feel ready to go.

"Where's that ice water?" I ask. I need to spray it over myself. It's by the tree. I grab it and hit the back of my neck with the cold liquid. But it doesn't do squat. When I come back, Ginny's standing upright.

"Alright?"

"Fine," I say. "I'm fine."

She doesn't look like she believes me. Her eyebrows go up and she's looking at the wetness of my shirt. Her eyes flicker back to my face and she purses her lips.

"You sure? If this morning was too much, tell me, I'll read-just the schedule. Or—"

She keeps talking and her voice runs over me. Its throaty purr sends images through my mind that shouldn't be there this early in the morning.

"I'm fine," I say in a choked voice. "Just ready for a shower."

I turn away. A cold shower. I wonder if she's going to wear those little shorts every morning. If so, the hardest part of the morning isn't going to be the exercises, it's going to be watching her in her tiny shorts ordering me around.

"Right. Okay," she says. "I'll leave the schedule with you then. For this afternoon and tonight."

"Sounds good."

I expect her to set it down and leave, but after she drops the clipboard next to the water bottle she hesitates.

"The reason I asked," she says. She stops and stays quiet. Finally I turn back to her.

"What?"

"About yesterday."

I shrug. "It's nothing."

"Okay. I guess. It's just, not that this is what happened with you, but after my husband died...I couldn't sleep."

"Yeah. No. I'm sorry, that's not it." I cross my arms over my chest and lean against the tree. I don't elaborate. Now she'll go.

She wipes a drop of sweat from her brow and sighs.

"Okay." She turns halfway then stops. Smiles, a sweet smile that makes me want to keep her here just so I can see more of it. "Sorry, it's stupid. I just need to say it. I almost died, no it's fine"—she waves me back—"I was drowning, and there was a moment before I lost consciousness where my body relaxed and I felt completely at peace."

I wonder if this is the time Bean wrote about in her letter. There's a hollow leaden feeling in my stomach.

"Okay," I say. Which I realize sounds completely idiotic.

She gives me a rueful smile.

"So, every time I started to fall asleep, when my body relaxed and my mind started to drift to sleep, something inside me would trigger and I'd be pulled back under, and all of a sudden I was back trapped in the car, drowning and a second away from death. I couldn't sleep, for years, sleep was just as terrifying as dying."

I look down at my feet. "What did you do?"

"Years of therapy. Meditation. Medication. Vitamins. Acupuncture. Anything and everything to make it stop."

"And?"

"And one day, I realized that it hadn't happened in a week. Then, it hadn't happened in months. And finally, I can count the time in years."

"So, you're saying that I won't always be afraid of heights."

She doesn't respond right away, so I look up. I catch her eyes with mine, but then my gaze travels to her mouth. It's bright pink from all our exercise and I don't want to think about heights anymore, I want to think about kissing her.

"No," she says. "I don't know what'll happen for you. I'm just saying I understand."

I nod. She understands.

"See you tomorrow." She lifts her hand in goodbye.

"Tomorrow," I say.

I watch her as she walks back to her beater car. She's got trim legs, a pert behind, a voice of honey, a will of iron, and enough baggage that not even the superhero Liam Stone would be able to lift.

"Not for you," I tell myself. A sometimes-crazy widow with a sick kid is not dating material. Not even if she makes me feel alive again.

I sigh and head back to the trailer for a cold shower.

8

Ginny

*B*ean can hardly contain her excitement. "Where are we going? Are we there yet?"

Liam shakes his head and I grin. "Surprises aren't her forte," I say.

He called this afternoon and said he scheduled Bean's first official training session for five thirty. It worked for me, so now we're on our way to the mystery location. Bean's strapped into her car seat and I'm in the passenger seat of Liam's posh car. I felt bad cramming her devil car seat with its juice stains and sharp plastic edges onto the soft leather backseat, but he didn't seem to mind.

Bean leans forward and says for the seventeenth time, "Are we there yet?"

When Liam sends her an incredulous look I try and fail to smother my laugh.

We've only been in the car for three and a half minutes, so I sympathize with him. I really do.

He turns left onto Route 511B.

"Are we going swimming in the old quarry?" asks Bean.

That's a good deduction. We don't usually head this way unless we're going swimming. The county filled in the quarry pit and made it a public park years ago. There are ledges to dive off and a little pebble beach with picnic tables.

"Nope," says Liam.

I don't know where we're headed either. Bean may not like surprises, but they used to be one of my favorite things. As a kid, when everyone else in school snooped to find out their Christmas presents, I savored the surprise and never wanted to know. That pleasure faded once I grew up, but now I'm feeling the joy of anticipation again.

I look over at Liam. He has next day stubble on his jaw, and his hair is messy, but he looks rested and there's a sort of excited energy coming off him. Bean's grilling him with her twenty questions routine and he's holding his own. The right edge of his mouth quirks and I think he's trying not to smile.

As Bean chatters happily and Liam gets in a yes or a no I lean back into the warm leather seat and find myself starting to relax. Someone else is driving, Bean's happy, and right now, in this moment, I don't have to do anything but go along for the ride.

I watch Liam out of the corner of my eyes. He laughs at something Bean says and then Bean laughs too. A warm glow fills me and I want to capture it and bottle it up so I can take it out later.

"No. We're not about to fight The Spider. I beat him, remember?" says Liam.

"Then are we going to Stone Mountain?" asks Bean. She doesn't wait for an answer. "No. That's in the Arctic, we couldn't drive there," she says to herself. "Unless, are we going to the airport?"

I glance over at Liam. Finally, the smile he's been holding back gets away from him and he grins. "Not today."

"Are we there yet?" she asks.

"Just about."

Bean cheers.

Then Liam pulls into the large, nearly empty parking lot of the archery center.

"Wow," says Bean when she realizes where we are. "I'm going to learn to shoot. I'm going to learn to shoot, Mama! Just like Liam."

I raise an eyebrow at him and he winks.

Once inside, I realize that Liam rented the place out for the night. We have an instructor, a Bean-sized bow, and the archery range all to ourselves.

"You should try it too," says Liam.

He's holding a bow out to me. "I don't know," I say. "I'm not really a bow and arrow kind of person."

"Come on, Mama. If you don't learn, then we'll have to rescue you from a villain. And that's so lame." Bean gives me an exasperated look.

Liam coughs into his fist. I glare at him, because he's obviously laughing at me.

"True," I say. "That would be so lame."

Liam coughs harder and I smirk at him.

So it's settled. I'm going to learn to shoot too.

Bean's in awe when she realizes that Liam had all the bad guys from the comics and movies printed out for the targets. I'm in awe when I realize that she's a natural and her aim is perfect.

"You're a natural," I say. "This is amazing."

I clap when she hits another. After Bean makes a dozen shots, Liam steps next to me.

"She's amazing," I say.

"That she is," says Liam, but he's looking at me.

"Um, I..." I blush and awkwardly heft the bow in my hands. Liam looks at it and seems to remember that I'm supposed to be shooting too.

"Your turn. Give it a go."

"Alright," I say.

He gestures to the range. He shot before Bean did. His arrows are bullseye in the farthest targets. When he loaded the bow I was surprised at the bunching of his shoulder muscles and the steadiness of his aim. I didn't think that he'd actually shot in his movies, but clearly he did, and he didn't lose his touch.

I listened carefully while the instructor laid out what to do, but I'm still not quite sure how it all works. When I let the arrow fly it sort of skitters through the air and then flops to the ground.

"That was pretty bad," calls Bean from across the range.

"Thanks, kiddo."

"You could try again," she says.

I do, and the second time's even worse. On my third try the arrow bounces off the wrong target. Bean realizes that archery is apparently the one physical activity that I'm not naturally talented at.

She works with the instructor on technique and is soon happily absorbed in hitting all the targets dead center.

Liam stands next to me. We're quiet as we watch Bean shoot and then cheer when she hits a villain.

"So, you're pretty terrible at archery," he says.

I pretend to be affronted.

He rubs his chin and gives me a contemplative look. "I figured you were good at everything you set your mind to. I mean, what's a measly archery target compared to an unsuspecting actor minding his own business..."

"Hey now," I say. I elbow him in the side and he laughs.

"Come on, I'll help you." He gestures for me to stand next to him. I move closer and he motions me closer still. I do, and I try not to notice the way I react to his nearness.

He's changing. It's been such a short time and he's already regaining the parts of himself that made him such a success. Or maybe it's me. I was so focused on getting his help for Bean that I ignored the way my stomach flutters when he looks at me.

"Hold up your bow," he says.

I hold it up and my arms shake. Not because it's too heavy, but because he's so close. I take a breath to steady myself and I can smell the clean fresh scent of the soap he uses.

"Not like that," he says. "Can I?"

"Okay," I say. He moves his hands to my arms and runs them over me. I stand perfectly still and try not to let on what his touch is doing to me. He's the first man to touch me in years.

"You alright?" he asks. His lips are near my ear and I fight not to rock back toward him.

"Good," I say. My voice is tight and my muscles strain against the lock I have on them.

"Relax your stance a bit," he says. "Lean back toward me."

I let go a whisper more and move another inch toward him.

"That's better," he says. There's a husky note to his words and I fight not to look back at him.

"Now what?"

He moves his hands down my back and my hips. "Keep yourself in line," he says.

My eyelashes flutter and the bow wobbles in my grip.

"Whoa there."

"Sorry." I straighten the bow again.

"Pull it taut," he says. His deep voice vibrates over me and I can nearly feel his lips against the sensitive skin of my earlobe.

I draw the arrow back. The tension of the bow mirrors the tension in me. I'm so close to Liam that the heat of him flows over me. My stomach flutters and I ache to let the arrow go. To release.

"Find your target?" asks Liam.

"Yes," I whisper. I'm ready.

He exhales and his breath flutters through my hair and over my skin. I ache to stretch against him.

"Send it home," he says.

I let the arrow go. The power and tension of the bow shoots it forward. All the anticipation, the tautness, explodes out and the arrow flies through the air. Then, it hits the target with a hard thump. The contact echoes a clenching in my gut.

I drop the bow to my side. For a moment, Liam and I stay close. My heart pounds and I feel the energy coming off him. Then the moment ends and he steps back.

"You did it," he says. His voice is taut.

I turn around and smile up at him. I try to keep my face free of any of the heat I'm feeling.

I search his expression. What is it that we're doing here?

He gives me his Liam Stone smile. That flash of dimples and the ruefully curled lips.

"Good job," he says. His smile turns polite and friendly. No heat there. It's just me.

And really, it means nothing.

I mean, it's been more than six years since a man has touched me, even as casually as this. My oversized reaction doesn't mean anything. I'd react this way to any guy that took a moment to smile and do a kind deed. Truly.

"Guess I can do anything I put my mind to," I say, trying to take us back to lighthearted joking.

"Sure can," he says, and I think he's relieved that I'm ignoring what happened just now.

"Thanks for this." I gesture to Bean. "You have no idea how much it means."

"Nothing to it."

"Still."

He shakes his head. "It's nothing. I'm just trying to get my career back. Nothing more, nothing less."

The warmth that had been unfurling in my belly fizzles out. "Yep," I say. "I know."

And I'm just trying to make Bean happy. Nothing more, nothing less.

I can't make too much of any of this. As Grandma Enid would say, that would just lead to abject misery and a case of hellish disappointment.

9

Liam

"*L*et's get breakfast," I say.

It's six thirty a.m. and Ginny and I stand in the morning mist sifting over the field next to my home. The wet dew sparkles gray and silver against the green and brown of the late summer grass. Even though it's supposed to be eighty today and I'm sweating up a storm, the morning air is still cool.

I look over at Ginny. She's in her tiny spandex shorts, a sports bra, and a backless tank. Sure enough, there are goose-bumps on her arms.

"How about coffee?" I ask. "I peg you as a coffee drinker."

She does that thing I'm starting to love where she raises an eyebrow and lifts one corner of her lips. It's the look that means she's thinking something outrageous. She had it when she first knocked on my door, when she dumped cheap whiskey over me, and when she trussed me up in my costume, and...plenty of other times, but each one meant something good was coming.

"Alright," she says. "You've been a champ. You can have a cup of joe, and then a cooldown."

"I have to pay for my coffee with more exercise?"

She gives me *that look* and heads to her car. I happily follow, watching the sway of her hips as she walks away. I try to not think about how much I'm enjoying her company and how every morning I wake up at the crack of dawn actually excited to get up. Because she's coming.

It's like with her, I'm starting to feel again.

I shake my head. I don't want to think about it. Things will get complicated real fast if I pursue that line of thought. Right now I only need one thing on my mind, getting myself in shape and getting back to Hollywood. No detours.

Ten minutes later we pull up to an Airstream in a deserted parking lot. Ginny rolls down her window and leans toward the open window of the silver Airstream.

"Hey Mona. Nice morning isn't it? We'll have two large black coffees," she says.

"Hey ya, Gin." The woman, Mona, smiles at Ginny. She has big, red cheeks, big hair, and lots of blue eye shadow. She glances at me and her eyes go wide behind her glasses. "Well I'll be darned. You're that actor."

I put on my charm-the-pants-off-them smile. "A pleasure," I say.

"Well," she says. "I don't know about some folks, but I'd like to say that I didn't care for you in that dinosaur movie. Too much swearing."

"Uh..." I look over at Ginny and shake my head. Never in my life have I been in a dinosaur movie.

Mona shakes a cup at me. "And that alien movie. Why'd you have to go and do something so violent?"

"Erm..." I clear my throat.

Ginny snickers into her hand.

"Bill, come out here," says Mona. A small man shuffles into view. "Look, it's that actor fella living out on the old Ridley Farm like a hermit. He's taking up with Ginny Weaver."

A bright blush springs up on Ginny's cheeks. "Oh no, Mona. I'm just his personal trainer. He needs to get fit for a movie role."

"Well, I never," says Mona.

I cough to cover up a laugh. Mona fans herself and I think that she and Ginny have a different idea of what "personal trainer" means.

Bill pokes his head out of the window. "I sure loved you in *Spiderman*," he says.

"Um, I didn't—"

"You mean that rated R one? That one with all the violence?" asks Mona.

I try not to drop my head into my hands.

"Wait 'til the boys hear that I saw Spiderman," Bill says.

Ginny's shoulders start to shake. Her face is beet red and she's pulled her mouth down, she's trying so hard not to laugh.

"Thanks for the coffee," I say.

"On the house," says Mona. "Just try not to do so much violence and swearin' in the future."

"I'll try my best, ma'am," I say.

The coffees are handed over and we pull away.

At a stop sign, Ginny snorts, then she starts laughing and can't seem to stop. She pulls in a breath and wipes at her eyes.

"Oh my gosh. You shoulda seen your face. They were bawling you out for a movie you didn't even do."

"They had no idea," I say.

We grin at each other and I think we'll go on looking at each other like this for a long time, but a car honks behind us.

Ginny looks back to the road and pulls forward.

At Route 511B she turns left.

"Where we going?" I ask.

"It's a secret," she says.

"Are we there yet?" I ask.

She swats at me and I laugh.

"I'll show you 'there yet,'" she says.

I smile then settle back and watch her drive. Every once in a while I take a sip of hot black coffee. Mona and Bill really know how to make a good brew. I usually like coffee full of cream, but this is good enough to not need anything.

The mist has cleared and the dashboard clock says it's nearly seven a.m. The soft light spills over the rounded tree tops and the hills. Ginny's still flushed and full of color. Morning looks good on her.

The car slows and Ginny turns onto a wide gravel road. She follows it for a half-mile and then pulls into a parking lot with wooden railroad ties that mark out spots.

"We're here," she says.

I climb out of the car after her. My muscles protest, so I stretch them out as I take in the shrill sound of a bird and the fresh smell of summer woods. There's a honeysuckle bush nearby sending out a sweet sugary scent.

Ginny walks toward me and the gravel crunches under her shoes.

"Where are we?" I ask.

She tilts her head toward a narrow dirt path at the edge of the woods. "Come on."

She looks back at me to make sure I'm following. I'm not yet, but I do when she gives me her smile.

She jogs through the trees and I keep up with her. We already ran today. Ginny was worried that too much running would hurt my hip and back, but I consulted with my doctor and I'm all clear to go. It feels good to stretch out my legs. The dirt of the trail kicks up behind us.

Then, when I'm about to ask if we're there yet, the woods open up and I stop at the edge of a stone ledge.

"Wow," I say.

Ginny takes in my expression. "You like it?"

"It's incredible."

Ten feet below us is a lake. The water is morning smooth, not a ripple on its surface. The deep blue of the sky, white clouds, and the green of the surrounding trees reflect on its surface. I peer down, the two of us are reflected in the water, standing on top of the jutting white ledge. A mallard and his mate call out and bank overhead, then land in the lake. The water splashes against their beating wings, then ripples around them and spreads out until the ripples hit the rocky edge.

"Can we?" I ask. I don't even think about the fact that jumping is a lot like falling. And if I do jump, it'll feel just like it did before.

Because, I'd like to dive in just like that mallard.

Ginny nods. Then she grabs the bottom of her tank and lifts it over her head. She drops it on the rocks. My mind goes blank. She's beautiful.

I take in the smoothness of her skin, and the flare of her stomach to her hips. She kicks off her shoes. She has the most delicate, the cutest little toes. I want to kiss each of them. Suddenly, I'm in motion. I don't want to be left behind. I pull off my shoes and my shirt and kick them into a pile.

When I look back at Ginny, her eyes are on my chest. There's a strange look on her face. I look down, is there something wrong? But no, it's still me. Although maybe a little flatter than a few weeks ago. But it's still me.

I look back up at her.

She's backed up a few steps and her knees are bent. There's a glint in her eyes.

"Last one in," she says.

My eyes go wide and she starts to run.

60

"Runs three miles," she says as she darts past me.

She laughs and I charge after her. I don't think about heights or fear or breaking bones. The only thing on my mind is chasing after her and catching that laughter.

We both reach the edge at the same time. I grab her hand.

I whoop as we fly through the air. Our fingers tangle and then we're falling. My stomach rushes up to meet my throat. But my throat doesn't close on me. I squeeze her fingers.

Then we hit the water. The cold catches us and we plunge deep into the lake. I lose Ginny's hand. I open my eyes. Air bubbles float around me, there's lake weed. Ginny kicks to the surface and I follow. I burst to the top and pull in air.

She treads water next to me and I swim toward her.

"We tied," she says.

I do a few strokes to swim closer. The water's deep here. At least fifteen feet, and we're about twenty feet from a low ledge. The water's choppier now, stirred up by our jump and treading.

It's only sinking in now that I jumped and fell and I didn't panic. I check to see if my chest is tight or if there's any numbness spreading through my limbs. Nothing.

I look at Ginny in amazement. I did it. We did it.

Does she realize?

She gives me a small smile.

Yeah. I think she does.

"Alright. Play time's over," she says. "Give me ten laps."

I look to see if she's joking, but she's dead serious.

"Yes, ma'am," I say.

While I swim freestyle across the lake and back, Ginny lays out on the ledge and warms herself in the rising sun. Every time I swim away I think about catching a glimpse of her long legs. Every time I swim back I take extra breaths to sneak a peek. I can feel her watching me too. And I like it. She's looking at me like I'm worth watching.

At ten laps I pull myself up on the ledge next to her. The water floods her spot on the rock.

"Hey. I just got dry," she says as she scrambles up.

"That so?" I stand and shake off. My hair flings drops all over her skin.

She raises her eyebrow, and right when I think, uh oh, she pushes me back in. I grab her hand as I fall and she drops in right on top of me. When we come up she sputters and wipes at her eyes.

I laugh at the look on her face. "Fair's fair," I say.

"Guess I deserved that," she says.

"Meh. Maybe I'm just a villain."

"Nah. I think you're better at playing the hero," she says.

A lightness fills me. But also a warning. Am I getting too close to her? Becoming too dependent on her? After only ten days?

She swims to the ledge and grabs the rocks with her hands, but she doesn't pull out of the water. She just holds herself there, hanging on, looking at the rock wall.

I realize that I've been thinking how jumping in was a triumph for me, but what about her. Didn't she say that she nearly drowned?

I swim up next to her and look at her profile. She doesn't look sad or scared. I actually can't read her expression.

Water drips down her face and I lift my hand to wipe it away, but then stop myself.

"How do you still swim?" I finally ask.

She looks at me, and her eyes crinkle into a smile. "I've never been afraid of swimming," she says. "Just drowning."

"And sleeping?"

"Not anymore."

I pull myself up onto the ledge and the cold water sluices off me.

I hold out my hand and she takes it. I pull her up next to

me. She's strong enough that instead of flopping like a fish onto the rock she steps up all graceful and poised.

"I wouldn't think you're scared of anything anymore," I say.

Her head jerks toward me and her eyes widen. "Everyone is scared of something."

She starts to climb the path toward the upper ledge where our shirts and shoes are. She puts on her tank and her shoes and I follow suit. The cloth of the tee sticks to my wet skin, and my shoes barely slip on.

I don't want to ask her what else she's scared of. I think I know.

Maybe I'm already in too deep. Because more than anything, I want to take all her fears away.

10

Ginny

Two weeks of training pass. Every morning I get up at four thirty and make it to Liam's by five. Grandma Enid, bless her, agreed when the early morning trainings started to watch Bean and give her breakfast in my absence. Although, she did make it very clear what she thought of my plan. Specifically, that I was driving down the road to hell and tarnation.

I'm beginning to agree with her. Why did I take him to the swimming quarry? Why did I let him hold me at the archery range? Why do I open up to him and share?

He's leaving. This is temporary.

Grandma Enid is right in a way. She thinks that hell and tarnation is getting Bean's hopes up, but the real hell is me starting to feel again. To think that I could have happiness. That Liam and Bean and I could...what? Nothing. We could nothing.

This happiness and hope, it will be what destroys me. Because nothing can ever come of any of this.

I had another appointment with Bean yesterday. She vomited when they put the needles in her back. I gave a brave face, let her hold my hand the whole while, her grip tight. But afterwards, when we got home, I told her to go paint models with Grandpa, and I took a shower. I sat on the floor, with my arms around my knees, the water running over me, and I felt like I was breaking in half. I let my sobs fall into the drain, they broke out of me, I couldn't stop them anymore. I couldn't hold it in, so I let them come. Then, when my stomach ached from it all, I stood up and let it fall away. I tucked it aside, got dressed, and went and made Bean a ham and cheese sandwich.

I kissed her head. Made her drink her milk. Praised her painted tank model, told a joke, made her feel loved and safe.

That's all I can do.

It's another morning of training. I left Bean curled up under her covers, sound asleep. Grandma Enid was making pancakes in the kitchen. She's given up the lectures, she just waved her spatula as I left.

Liam was waiting for me on his porch when I arrived.

So far, I have nothing to complain about. He works hard and does all the exercises I demand. I ask for one hundred push-ups, he does two hundred. I ask for fifty sit-ups, he does seventy-five. He seems even more determined than me to get back in shape. Most evenings he swings by to take Bean and I out for superhero training. To Bean's delight after the archery range we went to the park for rock climbing, horseback riding, and the library to check out books (because a superhero's greatest weapon is her mind). Every time Liam comes by, he has a new lesson planned for Bean. She's glowing lately, so high on life.

It's all thanks to Liam.

The sun's just rising over the trees. The birds sing and last autumn's leaves crunch under our feet. I let my legs propel me forward. I love running. The reason I became a trainer was because in the worst of times, running forward, that solid pounding of my feet on the ground was the only thing that kept me going.

Liam looks back at me and smirks. Sweat drips down his face and he wipes at it. I wave at him and motion him on. He turns back and runs on.

I try to fit in two hours' worth of exercise in the morning before it gets too hot and humid. At night, I have a routine that Liam does on his own. Right now, we're on our daily trail run, it's three miles through the woods. We follow a narrow hiking trail through a county park near Liam's property.

I run behind him. He's already stripped out of his shirt. His back muscles flex as he jumps over a stump. There's a stream ahead and he clears it in a leap. My legs aren't as long so I skip on a mossy stone and hop to the opposite bank. Cool air rises up from the stream and I take in the smell of cool water, mud, and summer leaves.

We run down a short steep hill. I'm distracted looking at his shoulders, so I'm not as careful as I should be. I slide in loose dirt. I can't stop my momentum.

I yelp as I fall, then I smack into Liam. My hands slide down his bare back. He's covered in sweat and my hands slip on the smooth wetness of his skin.

"Sorry."

He turns and grabs my arms. Steadies me.

My breath is heavy and labored. His hands still clutch my arms and suddenly I feel dizzy. He's breathing heavy too, and his chest rises and falls as he sucks in the morning air.

"No problem," he says. His fingers slowly curl over my arms, and he unconsciously tightens and loosens his hold on me. I don't move, I just stay in his grasp.

Then he gives me that heartbreaker smile that I've gotten

used to. The one that made women across the world fan themselves and clench their lady parts. I'd like to say I'm immune to it. But I can't. Even though I know it's only his movie persona smile, the one he gives when he's amused or trying to be charming, I'm not immune.

Finally, his expression changes. The morning sunlight sifts through the trees and turns his eyes from amused to something else.

"What?" I ask. I can't decipher the look he's giving me. Slowly, he lets go of my arms and reaches up to slip a strand of hair behind my ear. His fingers run over my skin as he tucks it in place. Strangely, him doing that feels more intimate than anything he's done before.

He swallows and I watch as a drop of sweat runs down his neck and falls down his bare chest.

I want to splay my hands over him. Run my fingers through his hair in exchange for what he did to me.

"Sorry," he says. "Sorry about that." He takes a step back.

I shake my head. Try to brush off the funny effect his touch is having. "No problem," I say. Then, "Shouldn't you be running?"

He grins then, and his amused expression is back in place. "You ever get tired of bossing me around?"

He starts out at a jog and I fall in behind him. The trail's too narrow to run side by side. Usually we don't talk, we just listen to the rhythm of our feet on the dirt. But today, something feels different, and now it's like the quiet would be more intimate than talking. So...

"Nah. It's why I'm a personal trainer, so I can yell at people all day."

He looks back at me as he chuckles, then quickly looks forward again. You have to pay attention when you're running on a trail, or risk tripping on a root and falling on your face.

"Why'd you become an actor?" I ask, when the silence lasts

too long.

"Oh, you know. So people can stare at me all day long."

I smile then realize he can't see me. "I bet," I say, but I don't believe him. "You don't care about that."

He looks back. "Sure I do." And he means it. His face is serious and a little sad.

"Really? You don't seem like that. You're not—"

"Big-headed?"

"No."

"Conceited?"

"No."

"Narcissistic?"

"No. You're definitely all those things."

"Hey," he says. He turns and gives me a look.

And I laugh, because none of that's true. He's none of those things.

We hit the end of the trail and turn to loop back to the beginning. The sun is just over the trees now and the forest is awake. Liam jumps over a log that lies across the trail and I follow. The sweet scent of damp earth and decomposing wood washes over me.

I glance at the shape of him. His back is strong and defined. His legs are gaining muscle. His hair is still overlong, but I like it.

"So what then?" he asks, as he glances back at me. "I'm not..." he prompts.

I smile. "You don't only care about yourself."

He stops, and I just catch myself before I run into him again. "Why'd you stop?"

He turns. "That's where you're wrong. I *only* care about myself."

"Come on," I push at him, start him running again so our legs don't cramp up. After a hundred yards of running I say, "I see you with Bean. You're amazing. That means you care."

"About myself," he says, almost like he's talking to himself. The muscles in his back are stiff and he seems angry all of a sudden.

"What's that supposed to mean?" I ask. I don't understand the sudden change in his mood.

"I need to get something clear," he says. He turns back to me. He looks conflicted and angry.

"Okay," I say. "Feel free."

He turns again, then faces forward.

"I'm not doing this for you."

"I know."

"Or your daughter."

I flinch. "I know that too."

"I'm doing it for me, I want to get back to Hollywood."

Okay, it hurts to hear him say this, but I already knew all this. "I know," I say more forcefully than before, and maybe with a trace of bitterness.

His shoulders bunch up. He looks back at me again, and a cloud passes over his face. He turns forward then says, "Just so we're clear. You're a means to an end, yeah?"

Suddenly, my throat hurts and I swallow the burning sensation down. "You're an ass," I spit out. I don't know what's gotten into him, but he's being an ass.

He looks back. I'm about to yell at him about keeping his eyes on the darn trail when he trips on a root. He twists and slams to the ground. He hits the dirt and skids on his side along the trail.

I can't stop running in time and my feet get tangled in his legs. I land on top of him.

The air is knocked from me. I roll to the dirt and try to pull in air. Little stars dance in my eyes and my lungs ache for breath. Finally, after what feels like an eternity, I draw in air. Thank the Lord.

Liam props up on his elbows and looks down at me with concern.

"You alright?"

His jerk mood seems to have dissipated with the fall.

I shake my head and relax back into the dirt. "Give me a minute."

He lays down next to me and we stare up at the leafy canopy. There's a squirrel on a tree limb that looks down at us and chatters. After a few twitches of its tail it scatters away.

"Sorry I was an ass," Liam finally says. He clears his throat and looks over at me.

I shake my head but don't say anything for a moment. Then, "What was that all about anyway?"

He props his hands under his head and gazes up at the sky. Finally, "I don't want you to think I'm more than I am."

He's tense and I suddenly understand. He's warning me that he's leaving and he doesn't want me to get too attached. Or to make this more than it is.

I sigh. How did this get so complicated so quickly? He was supposed to be a guy that would help Bean have her wish come true. He wasn't supposed to be anything *more*.

"Believe me. Two weeks ago, I poured whiskey on your drunk head. I'm not going to think you're more than you are." I pucker my lips. That tasted like a lie.

"Yeah, but sometimes, the way you look at me..." He stops and turns to look up at the sky again.

My cheeks burn with embarrassment.

He props himself up on his elbow. "I don't know what to think. I just want to make clear that all I want out of this is to get back to Hollywood."

"Okay."

"I don't want any misunderstandings."

"Got it."

"Sometimes I think you're picturing me as your daughter's substitute dad or your fantasy husband. I can't be that."

I push up and scramble back away from him. "What's wrong with you today?" An angry bloom fills my chest. I lash out. "I've already had a husband, *Liam*. And he was a helluva better man than you'll ever be."

Tears sting my eyes. I stand up and start down the trail. Away from him.

He jogs after me and catches up. I keep running and don't speak. Running has always been my way to soothe anger, fight fear, and keep moving forward. I use it now.

A half-mile from the road the trail widens. Liam runs next to me.

"Hey," he says.

"What?" I snap. Enough already. Yes, I'm getting too attached. Yes, I'd be ecstatic if my daughter weren't dying and I had a husband who loved me. He doesn't have to rub it in.

He slows down and then stops running.

After a few steps, I stop and turn. "What?" I'm tired and I want to head back home. I have to shower, eat, spend some time with Bean, and get to work by nine.

He looks at me and I try not to look too pissed off. Unfortunately, what makes me most angry is I realize he's right. I've been idolizing him, thinking of how much Bean likes him, how he makes her happy. How he might make me happy.

I wasn't thinking of what he wants.

"I'm sorry," he says.

"For what? You were just telling the truth."

He shakes his head and starts to speak, but I cut him off.

"Do you want to know something?"

"Okay," he says. He steps closer. I avoid his eyes and instead look over his shoulder at the green and brown of the woods.

"Bean would love it if you were her dad. There's nothing

that would make her happier. And that would make me happy."

I catch the slight shift in him as his shoulders stiffen. It hurts. I close my eyes against it and continue. "Why would I tie myself to a man I met only a few weeks ago? Why would I fantasize about something that can never exist? It's not real and it never will be real. You might not know it, but I do. I've accepted it. Bean may not grow up. I may never see that. I already know this. I already know." It sits heavy on my chest every hour of every day.

"I'm sorry."

"Stop it. Don't...I don't need a husband, or a father for Bean. I need a hero. Okay? I need you to be a hero. Effin' Liam Stone."

I finally look up at him and realize he's been watching my face. "Okay."

"No matter how you think I'm looking at you, or how much you think I want you, I don't. Because it's not real."

"Okay." Something changes in his expression and then something shifts in him too.

I look at him, and he stares at me. His dark stubble lines his jaw and his eyes search mine. There's something unspoken here between us. This quiet awareness that both of us are too scared to admit. Neither of us makes the first move. But the tension between us grows thick and heavy. His eyes flick to my mouth. My lips tingle under his gaze.

"You don't want me," he says.

"No," I say.

His eyes stay on my lips.

"Not for a husband."

"Never."

"Not for a substitute father."

"Not at all."

"You just want to train."

"That's right."

I swallow as his eyes go darker and his lids lower. His hands curl and my skin tingles as I imagine him touching me again.

"There's nothing here," he says.

"Nothing at all."

He studies me for a moment. The only sound is a woodpecker tapping at a tree. I stand still under his gaze. Then, "I have to kiss in my movies."

We're both crazy. There's no other explanation. Because I'm not surprised at all that he said this.

I nod, and it feels like I'm moving through syrup, the air is thick and sweet. It's only natural that he'd mention kissing. His eyes go heavy and dark as he watches my mouth.

"I might need to add it to my training. Kissing."

"Mmmhmm," I say.

"Because you don't want me. There's no risk of misunderstandings."

"Not at all," I say.

He leans forward and I lean toward him.

"How would I do it, if we were in a scene together?" he asks.

I look at his mouth, the dip in his lower lip, and his strong chin.

I clear my throat. "You'd put your hands..."

He steps only inches from me and I feel the heat coming off him. "On your shoulders?"

"This isn't a junior high dance," I say.

He smiles and I tilt my head up to look at him.

"You'd put them on my hips."

He reaches down and presses his fingers into the curve of my hips. "Like that?" he asks.

His palms spread out and he rocks me closer. "Perfect," I say. My voice is throaty and I sway toward him.

"Then what?" he asks.

"Then you'd brush your lips over mine. Lightly. Just a taste."

He bends his head down and runs his lips over mine. I open my mouth to him and lick at the salty flavor of him.

"Like this?" he whispers.

"That's right."

"Now what?"

I trace my lips over his and he pulls me closer. "You open my mouth with yours and—"

He doesn't let me finish. His lips close over mine and he teases my mouth open. He sucks on my lips, and runs his hands over my hips, and sends his tongue into my mouth and I'm breathing hard and my hands are on his bare shoulders and I'm not standing anymore but pulled up against him and I wrap my legs around him and I'm...he carries me over to a tree and pushes me against it. Then he starts to move over me and I'm pressed between the tree and the hardness of him.

I kiss him and kiss him and kiss him like I'll never ever kiss anyone ever again. My fingers dig into his shoulders and I can hear little noises and I realize it's me. He tugs at my hair and pulls me in closer and reaches one hand up to run it along my ribs and up toward my breast and he almost there. Then his hand curls up over the bottom of my breast and his hand rests on me, he flicks a finger over a nipple and I cry out into his mouth. He captures my cry and presses harder into me, takes my mouth like he'll never let me go. I don't want him to. I don't...he yanks his mouth free, jerks back and drops me to the ground.

My knees buckle, and my legs nearly give out. My head swims, but I manage to right myself. I pull in a hard breath. My heart pounds and I try to reorient myself. But the whole world is skewed now and I can't find north.

I look to Liam. His back's turned and he's breathing hard.

What happened?

What the heck was that?

Liam still hasn't turned around. The heat that poured through me is gone. I rub at my arms.

A hawk screeches overhead and I'm pulled back into reality.

I have work in less than an hour. I'm a widow scrambling to keep my head above water and get my sick daughter to her treatments every week. I also want to give my daughter her one dream. Which doesn't include me making a fool of myself for a temperamental movie star.

"Alright then." I say, and I'm proud because my voice is normal. "I think you've got it down."

Understatement.

He runs a hand through his hair and finally turns to me. His cheeks are red, but otherwise he looks exactly the same as he always does. Except, well, more toned. He's more toned by the day.

"Ginny—"

"Training's done for the day." I say. "I don't think we need to do that again." Then I run past Liam. I don't want to talk about it. About that *kiss*.

It only takes three minutes to finish the last half-mile.

"I have to get to work," I say. I'm out of breath from the fast half-mile. I reach for my car door. I know it looks like I'm running away, but I don't care.

This morning got away from me and if I ignore it maybe we can go back to the way things were.

"I'll see you tonight," says Liam.

"No." I shake my head. "You don't need to. I'll see you tomorrow morning."

He puts his hand on the door to my car to stop me from opening it. "We'll have dinner."

My face must betray my shock.

"Not a date," he says. "I have another lesson for Bean."

Oh. Right. Right.

"Gotcha." I close my eyes and try to push away all the reactions I'm having to him. Just to make things clear between us, I say, "I'm not looking for a husband."

I wait for his reaction. When he doesn't have one I say, "Or a substitute father."

"Yeah."

"We shouldn't have kissed," I say, although that tastes like a lie. Especially since I'd like him to lift me up again and start where we left off.

He doesn't argue.

In fact, he doesn't say anything at all. He just looks at me with the strangest expression on his face.

I drive off. But it feels like I'm still running.

11

Liam

I show up at Ginny's garage door entrance at six o'clock. I knock and clasp the bouquet of daisies in my hand. They're a little scraggly and weedy looking, but Centreville doesn't have a florist. So I spent a half-hour wading through the tall grass on the side of Route 511 collecting the daisies that grow there. I'm more nervous than I was before my first audition, and I don't know why. I just want to apologize. Flowers in hand.

This morning, I was feeling things for Ginny that I don't have any right to feel. I'm not a good bet and I'm not sticking around. At first I thought that Ginny was the one with all the baggage and that was the reason I wanted to avoid her. Now I realize she's dealt with her past, it's me that can't move forward. In fact, I want to head back to the past and live in it. Hollywood, here I come.

The door to Ginny's garage apartment remains shut. The flowers are starting to sag. I knock again then use my sleeve to brush at the sweat dripping down my face. The full sun glares down and the black pavement of the drive is hot.

"Eww. Is that loser giving Ginny flowers?" Someone makes gagging sounds. My neck prickles with embarrassment and I turn around. It's that little bully Redge. He's with the teen Finick and Heather. I recognize Heather from the day she came by the trailer. She's wearing a tight dress and high heels. There's a sneer on her face. Then she notices the flowers in my hand and the fact that I'm standing at Ginny's door. Her eyes narrow.

"Ha," says the man with them. He has a long narrow head with a sharp chin, pleated pants, tassel shoes, and a gold watch. He slaps Redge on the back. "Good one, son."

"Stoney," Heather purrs. They walk up to me. Heather looks at the flowers in my hand and smirks. "Looking for someone?"

I don't want to say anything that could be misconstrued. I get the feeling that there's no love lost between this family and Ginny.

The man looks between me and Heather and finally seems to realize that Heather and I have met before.

"Heather, you know him?"

Heather gives a little smile. "Stoney and I used to work together. He *was* an actor."

Comprehension lights in his eyes and he slaps his thigh. "Oh, right. Ha ha. You're the has-been hero. That coo-coo comic guy. The wash-up everyone makes fun of." He chortles and little Redge snickers. Then he leans toward Heather and says under his breath, "Didn't you say he was a drunk?"

My jaw clenches and a little lead ball settles in my chest.

He turns back to me. "I'm Joel Wilson, mayor of Centre-ville." He holds out his hand to shake. Then he realizes the bouquet of daisies are in my right hand. He gives me a hard look.

"You're not bothering Ginny, are you?"

"What?" I'm sort of shocked with his sudden turn from put-downs to hostility.

He points to the door. "Ginny. She's like family."

"She's not family," says Finick. He's been trying to ignore us all up to this point.

Joel doesn't pay any attention to him. "I don't want to hear you're bothering her. She has enough trouble."

Heather sighs and rolls her eyes. "My word, Joel. Enough with the protectiveness over Ginny."

"I'm hungry," says Redge.

Just then the front door of the house opens and the pickle grandma pokes her head out. Her eyes widen. "Clark, they're here," she shouts back in the house. Then she sees me and she looks to the sky and shakes her head. "Ginny," she shouts through the door, "that superhero fella is here." Then she steps onto the sidewalk and gestures for us to come up to the house. "Come on, y'all. What are you doing standing out in the heat? You'll wilt like...why do you have a handful of weeds?"

She's looking at the wilted daisies. Half the petals are gone and the heads droop down. Redge starts to snicker again.

Finick lets out a long sigh and moves past to get into the air conditioning of the house.

"A kiss first, Finick," says the grandma. He slumps his shoulders and gives her a peck on the cheek. "You too, Redge," she says. After she's had all her hugs and kisses she stands on the porch and crosses her arms over her chest.

I'm not sure if she wants me to kiss her too. I smother a laugh at the thought. Just then Bean runs out the door.

"You're here," she shouts. She barrels into my legs and gives my waist a tight squeeze. "I'm so excited. What're we doing? Where are we going?"

I grin and pat her head. When I look up, Ginny's standing on the porch watching the two of us. I think my heart must be in my eyes because who can't love Bean? But I see my words from earlier today in Ginny's gaze. No misunderstandings.

I wait until Bean disentangles herself. Then I step back. "It's a surprise."

"Oh, boy. Mama says surprises aren't my forte."

I hold back a smile. "Well, one thing about superheroes is we have a lot of patience."

"Hmm." She considers this then seems to discard it because right away she asks, "But where are we going?"

I grin.

"You're not going anywhere until you eat your dinner, Beatrice."

"But, Grandma, maybe Liam is taking us to dinner. Are you taking us to dinner?"

"Well—"

"It's family dinner night," Bean's grandma says. She gives Ginny a pointed look, then she strolls into the house, leaving the door open behind her. I can feel the cold chill of the air conditioning.

Ginny steps down. "Sorry, I forgot about the dinner. I'm sure you don't want to join us, we could—"

"I'd love to."

"What?"

"I'd love to."

Bean jumps up and down and cheers. "Hooray. Then we'll go on the surprise. And I bet I'm gonna learn to fly."

"Are those for me?" asks Ginny. She's looking at the flowers in my hand.

I clear my throat and shift uncomfortably under her steady gaze. "I um—"

"Wanted to say you were sorry."

"Exactly," I say. I smile and hand her the bouquet. "They're not much. I mean, they don't mean anything. Just sorry."

She smiles. "It's alright."

"Come on, Liam. We're having pot pie with real venison. Finick always says that's disgusting 'cause eating venison is like eating Bambi, plus deer have ticks, but Grandpa says kids gotta eat venison or they'll turn out wimpy, and then Heather says if Finick doesn't like it he can go hungry then Finick says—"

"Well, you might as well come in," Ginny says.

Bean keeps on talking, giving me the history of venison pot pie as we head toward the dining room. The dining table has a lace table cloth on top and fine porcelain china. Bean's grandma is hastily arranging another place setting for me.

"You'll have to sit on a stool," she says, then glares at me, like she's challenging me to complain.

"Thank you," I say.

She sighs and then looks at the flowers in Ginny's hand.

"Those'll need a vase," she says.

Ginny follows her into the kitchen. I stare at the swinging door and everyone left in the room stares at me.

Then the grandma starts talking and we can all hear her loud and clear through the door.

"Why in tarnation did he give you weeds?"

"He gave me flowers," says Ginny.

"That man isn't right in the head. Those are cowpoke road-side weeds, clear as day."

"It's the thought, Enid."

"You're on the road to hell and tarnation. Heather warned you he's not fit to be around decent folk, much less Bean. Now he's here, sniffing around like a stray dog begging for a bone."

"Heather doesn't know squat."

At that, Finick snorts approvingly. "That's enough," Heather hisses at him.

"How's school?" asks Grandpa Clark.

"Grandpa, it's summer. We don't have school," says Bean.

"Oh, right, silly me."

But he's not really listening because Enid has started in on Ginny again.

"Heather is the daughter of my heart."

I can't make out what Ginny says. Instead, I move to the table and have a seat. The others move to it as well. The door to the kitchen swings open and Enid and Ginny come out smiling. Enid's smile is a little more forced than Ginny's. She sets the vase down in the center of the table with a flourish.

"And here are the lovely *flowers* for our centerpiece."

Clark says grace and then we pass around the pot pie. There's wine and Enid pours Joel and Heather a glass.

"I expect you're trying to cut down," Enid says to me.

Ginny looks over at me, her eyes wide.

"Sure enough," I say. I wink at Ginny and she blushes bright red.

"Liam," says Bean. She's bouncing in her chair, too excited to notice the undercurrents amongst the adults. "Are we gonna fly tonight?"

"Laud sakes," mutters Enid.

"You'll find out," I say.

"Or maybe we're gonna trace a villain to his hideout?"

A pea flies through the air and hits Bean in the face. "Hey," she says. She looks at Redge—he's using his spoon as a catapult.

"Ha ha," says Joel. "Now that's a clever boy. Future mayor there."

I can't believe that no one is reprimanding this boy. They are doing his future a terrible disservice.

"You need to apologize to Bean," I say.

Bean grins at me, and Ginny gives me a sweet smile.

Redge tightens his mouth mulishly.

"Go on, Redge," says Enid. "That was poor form."

I'm surprised, but apparently Redge knows who serves the dessert around here, because he blows out a breath in defeat.

"Sorry," he mumbles. He glares at me and Bean. She doesn't care though. She gives me a toothy smile.

I take a bite of the pot pie. It's steaming hot and gamey. Finick has avoided eating anything by strategically moving piles of it around his plate.

"So, what've you been doing with our Ginny and Bean?" Joel asks.

Everyone at the table turns to look at me, except Ginny, she looks down at the napkin in her lap.

"He's been training," says Bean. "And we've been shooting and climbing and we're gonna go flying."

"I'm surprised you've been able to stay upright for all that," says Heather.

"Ha," laughs Joel.

"He's been amazing," Ginny says in a tight voice.

Heather turns to Ginny and I see something petty spark in her eyes. "You do seem to get men to do *all sorts* of *things* for you. I wonder."

Enid's reaching for her glass, but at Heather's words her hand shakes and she knocks the wine to the table. The red spills across the cloth. Her face goes white and for a moment no one moves. Then she jumps back.

"So sorry," she says.

"I'll get a towel," says Ginny. She jumps up and runs to the kitchen. When she's back she sops up the spill.

"I'm sorry," says Ginny.

"You didn't do it," says Finick. He gives Heather a disgusted look.

"Know anything about modeling?" asks Clark. He glances at his wife, but Enid is still dabbing at the red stain.

"No, sir," I say.

He launches into a discussion about accurately modeling the Battle of Trafalgar. I try to listen attentively, but I keep glancing at Ginny. Her face is white and she's not looking up from her plate.

Heather leans toward her and I catch her whisper. "Looks like you've caught another one dead on the line."

Ginny flinches.

I can't let it pass. It's too much. "Excuse me," I say.

Clark stops talking and everyone looks at me in surprise. Ginny gives me a wary look, like she's not sure she wants to know what I'm about to say.

"Thank you for the lovely meal. And thank you for your concern about Ginny and Bean. I think you love them very much."

"Of course we do," cries Enid.

Redge snorts.

"I just have to say, you're lucky to have them. Because they're special. I've only known them two weeks and I can see that."

"Thanks, Liam," says Bean. She beams at me.

Ginny looks down at her plate.

"Of course we know they're special," says Joel. "That's why we look out for them. Don't want them making wrongheaded choices."

"They haven't," I say. I give everyone at the table a hard stare. "Ginny's the smartest, most determined, most caring person I've ever met. And Bean's the greatest kid I know. They wouldn't know how to make a bad choice."

No one says anything for a moment. Under the table, Ginny reaches over and lightly places her hand on top of mine. A load of tension falls out of me. She gives my hand a short squeeze.

"How about dessert?" asks Enid.

We eat apple crumble pie and talk about the Battle of Waterloo.

12

Ginny

*L*iam knocks down all the bottles in one throw.

"And we have a winner, folks," yells the carnival worker. "Winner, winner." Bright bulbs flare and a horn sounds.

Liam looks over to me and grins. I shake my head, mostly because of the cocky look on his face, but I can't help returning the smile.

"Yeah," shouts Bean. "Can I get the big bear? The big pink one?" She jumps up and down and points at a teddy bear that's bigger than she is.

"The little lady wants the bear," says the carnival worker with a sly look in his eyes. He holds out a fist-sized squirrel to Bean. "Here's the small prize. You need three wins for the big one."

"Ohh," says Bean. Her voice drops from high to low. "Erm, it's...hmm."

I start to laugh and Liam waves the prize away and hands over twenty dollars.

The worker grins and raises his microphone. "Player, player. We've got a big player."

Liam lightly tosses a ball in his hand.

"You can do it," says Bean. "'Cause you're—"

"Shhh," I say. I cut her off before she outs Liam.

"Oh yeah," she whispers.

I smile and tap her on her nose. Liam's surprise was bringing us to the county fair. Except, we're not here just to play carnival games, he and Bean are working on going incognito in alter egos. The rules are that no one can suspect they're a superhero and protégé.

He gave Bean a pink wig, a sequin hat, heart sunglasses and a shirt that says "superhero." I'm biased, since I'm her mom, but she looks so stinking cute I can barely stand it.

Liam raises the first ball and aims at the bottles. He pulls back and throws. He hits them, but only three fall.

"Tarnation. Those bottles are slippery as a mare in heat," he says. Then he turns and winks at me.

I hold back a laugh. He's fully in character. If I didn't know he was Liam Stone, I'd never recognize him. He has on a black cowboy hat, a fake mustache, cowboy boots, sunglasses and a shirt that says "I'm with stupid" with an arrow pointing at his face. Okay, fine, I start to laugh. He looks back at me and shakes his head. Then he tosses another ball at the bottles.

"Got 'er," he shouts and he pumps his fist in the air.

"So ridiculous," I say.

Bean jumps up and down and cheers. We're up to the medium prize, a stuffed taco with googly eyes and legs. Liam has two more balls to throw. The worker sets up the bottles and motions for Liam to take another throw.

"Player, player," the worker shouts into his microphone, "We've got a big player."

The midway is crowded. People mill about, try their hand at carnival games, eat cheesy chili fries, cotton candy or mysterious fried snacks on sticks. I take in the nostalgic smell of sugar, fried grease, and kicked up dust—those summertime fair smells. Of the hundreds of people passing by, not a one pays any attention to the movie star, aka down home cowboy, in their midst.

Bean grabs my hand. "You think he'll do it?" she asks. She's nearly bursting from excitement.

"Sure thing, honey," I say in a heavy twang. "He can hit a squirrel with a BB gun from a hundred paces. He can climb a tree, wrestle a bear, and jump off a cliff all in a single day. Ain't nuthin' he can't do."

Liam stops mid-throw and looks over at me. I wave him on. He shakes his head and looks at my outfit. I'm incognito too. Miniskirt, cowgirl boots, a red wig with a camo hat, sunglasses and a low-cut tank top that says "I get my kicks on Route 511B."

So ridiculous.

"Go on," I call. "Get 'er done."

He does. The ball hits the bottles and they collapse in a pile.

"Yeah," shouts Bean. She jumps up and down and claps and cheers.

"Boom," says Liam. "That, folks, is how it's done."

"Winner, winner, big winner," shouts the midway worker. The lights flash and the horn blares. The worker uses a long metal pole to grab the gigantic pink teddy, lasso it, and hand it down to Bean. She can't even wrap her arms around it, the teddy's so big.

"Here, I'll hold her for you," says Liam.

"Can we go on the Ferris wheel now?" asks Bean.

We absolutely can. It's nearing eight. The sky turns a dusty orange and blue and the midway lights wink on. The Ferris wheel sits at the end of the midway, next to the rocking Viking ship and the flying swings. We meander through the crowds and slowly make our way down.

"Thank you for the bear," I say.

Liam tips his cowboy hat. "Nuthin' to it."

Bean slips her hand into mine and my heart squeezes. I haven't had this much fun in...years. Who knew that dressing up in crazy outfits, and pretending to be someone else at the county fair could be so ridiculously fun? Not me.

"Am I doing good on my disguise?" asks Bean.

"Brilliantly," I say.

"The trick to being a superhero," Liam says, "is never letting people suspect what you are. You gotta keep all the good stuff hidden behind your alter ego." He looks Bean over. "You're doing good, kid."

"I thought so," she says and gives a satisfied smile. "You did good too."

"Thank you," he says. "I figured cowboy is a good disguise."

"No," Bean says. "I mean before. In your trailer, with your bathrobe and stuff. That was real good incognito."

I look over at the food trailers and pretend not to see Liam's dumbstruck look.

Finally, he nods. "Guess it was."

The line to the Ferris wheel is nearly fifty people long, but there's a cotton candy stand next to the line that's calling my name.

"You guys stand in line," I say. "I'm gonna get us some cotton candy."

"Purple please," says Bean.

She's in for a treat. I don't usually let her have much sugar, especially not this late at night. When she was first diagnosed I cut out sugar completely, but I loosened up a bit as time went by. It's hard not letting yourself have any sweetness.

After I grab the bag of cotton candy I make my way back.

Bean and Liam have moved forward a bit and I make my way toward their spot in the line.

When I reach them they're in the middle of a conversation and don't notice me. I stand behind them and wait for them to finish up talking.

"—never got to do that before. That's why I like you lots. Because we get to do fun things," Bean says. "'Cause Mama says I gotta save my energy, but Grandma says it's 'cause I'll break. So no more ball, or running, or rolling on the ground, and no more cartwheels especially, or sports. Redge says that makes me a baby, but Finick tells him to shut up. But I wish I could run still, cause my friends stopped wanting to play with me."

"That's too bad," says Liam. He looks down at Bean with a serious expression. "Sorry to hear that."

She gives a big nod. "Yeah. I don't have friends no more. I used to have friends but then they didn't like me not playing, 'cause I'm always tired. Then all my hair fell out and some kids made fun of me. Except Mira and Glen, but Mira moved to California and Glen's mom said he couldn't play with me anymore. And Mama tried to let me wear a hat to school but the principal said it's against the rules, so I didn't get to."

Liam looks down at Bean and I can tell he's struck by how much she can say in twenty seconds and how she doesn't seem to ever need to take a breath.

"Sorry, kid," he says.

"That's okay. I got my mama. She's real sad sometimes. She doesn't think I know, but I do. 'Cause I'm sick. She doesn't want me to die." Bean nods at Liam and her face is serious.

I lift my hand to my mouth. I didn't realize that Bean knew...

"Your mama loves you a lot," Liam says.

"That's why I got her you."

"What do you mean?" asks Liam.

"I figured, the only person that could make my mama

happy was you. 'Cause you're a hero, like my daddy. Can I hold my bear now?"

"Sure," says Liam. He hands the bear over and Bean squeezes it to her chest. Then he lifts up his sunglasses and wipes at his eyes.

I step forward and say in a bright voice, "Who wants purple cotton candy?"

"Me, me, me," says Bean.

"There you are," says Liam.

Neither of them say anything at all about the conversation they were having. When we make it to the front of the line we climb into the metal cage. Bean squeals as the cage rocks and we swing higher and higher up the Ferris wheel. When we reach the top, the wheel stops and we rock back and forth.

I can see so far. The lights of the fair beneath us, the animal barns and the midway, the expo, and the food stalls, then the valley and the hills and the town, and over the trees, the sun slips below the horizon.

Bean nuzzles between Liam and I, with her bear between her legs. I look over at Liam to see if he's watching the sunset. Instead, I realize that he's watching me. There's a funny expression on his face. It's like he's only just seen me, and he's not sure what to make of me. Or of anything.

I give him a hesitant smile. "You okay?"

His eyes flicker, then he gives me the world-famous Liam Stone smile. "Of course I am," he says.

The Ferris wheel starts up again and the moment passes. We descend back to the ground and then make our way home.

13

Liam

"*T*hanks for tonight," says Ginny.

"No worries."

Bean's asleep in the backseat, the bear in her arms and her face covered in purple cotton candy stain. Ginny lifts her out of her car seat. Bean makes a sleepy noise and then drops her head on Ginny's shoulder.

"I'll get the bear," I say quietly.

Ginny opens the door to her garage apartment. I stand at the threshold, not sure if I should drop the bear at the entrance or come in.

"Come on in," says Ginny. "Make yourself at home. I'll be out in a second."

While she washes up Bean and tucks her in bed, I go and sit on the living room couch. It's comfortable and there's a load of pillows and a quilt. I lean forward and look at the books on the coffee table. Ginny has a few physiology and sports medicine textbooks and there's a big pile of Liam Stone comic books. I flip through an issue and then lean back. Something pokes my leg and I pull out an action figure from the couch cushion.

"I recognize you," I say. It's the figure I pulled down from the tree. I toss it into a toy basket next to the couch.

I pick up the sound of Ginny singing a lullaby. Her voice is low and throaty, and she sings with quiet sweetness. I feel like an intruder. I shouldn't be here for this, it's not my place. There are pictures on the wall of Bean as a baby and as a toddler. It's a home, full of comfort and love, and I'm an imposter here.

I run my hand down the back of my neck and sigh. Then realize I'm still wearing my costume. I pull the mustache off my lip and tuck it in my pocket.

I should go.

I stand up and head toward the door. The kitchen's near the door on the back wall of the apartment. There's a single counter with a stove, a small refrigerator and a sink. The flowers I gave Ginny are the only thing on the counter. They're even more wilted than earlier. I stare at them and wonder what the heck I'm doing.

I flipped out this morning and made an ass of myself. I thought Ginny was going to get too attached, but it's not her I need to be worried about. It's me. I'm getting in too deep.

When she said she wasn't looking for a husband or a substitute father, I thought I'd be relieved, but I wasn't. It felt wrong, her saying that.

And then I kissed her. I wasn't thinking, I just knew I had to touch her, taste her. I'm starting to feel again and she's the reason behind it. I have to be careful. I'm leaving town. If I get too close, I won't leave a hero, I'll leave with a broken heart.

What'd Bean say? That she chose me because she knew I could make her mom happy?

I can't save the day. This situation is way beyond my fake powers.

"She's asleep," Ginny says. She looks at me standing at the door. "You're going?"

I nod. "It's an early morning. Five a.m." I reach toward the door.

"You could stay." I turn back to her and she gives me a hesitant half-smile. She's scrubbed her face clean of makeup and removed the red wig, but she's still in her miniskirt and tank top. I take in that half-smile and realize that this is way beyond just a physical want. I crave this woman.

"I don't think that'd be a good idea," I say.

Her smile drops from her face and she looks away. "I didn't mean...I wasn't inviting you..." She looks back up and her face is red. "I just thought we could hang out. As *friends*."

My gut clenches at the word "friends." I don't want to be her friend. Friends hang out, friends are platonic, friends don't do the things I'm fantasizing about doing to her.

"Friends?" I say.

She sighs and blows the hair out of her eyes. "Yes. Friends."

I put my hands in my pockets and lean back on my heels. She glances at the flowers on the counter.

Then she looks back to me and says, "I just want to get past the awkwardness of this morning. I get that you're not looking for a relationship. Heck, neither am I. That would be the worst thing I could do. Have you seen my life? I gotta give everything I've got to my kid. I don't have time for anything else."

As she's talking I notice the shadows under her eyes and the sagging in her shoulders. She's tired, a sort of bone-deep tired that I didn't notice before. Maybe it's because she's in her home and she's less on guard, but suddenly I can see how much she actually does need a friend.

Just a friend.

I make a split second decision. I can do that. I can be a friend to her. If I'm a friend, I won't leave a broken heart, I won't make anything complicated, nothing can go wrong if I'm only a friend.

"Got any movies?" I ask.

She looks up and her eyes are filled with happy surprise. "You'll stay?"

"Depends on what kind of movies you like," I say.

I follow her to the living room and we settle on the couch. She tucks her feet under her and her miniskirt rides up high. I pull my gaze back up from her long smooth legs to her face.

"What?" I ask.

"I said, I like horror. The scarier the better. Like pee-your-pants scary."

"That's the craziest thing I've ever heard."

She shakes her head. "Are you kidding? How can you not like them? The rules are set in horror movies. There's a monster. There's a sin. And there's punishment from the monster on anyone who sins."

"Like losing your virginity?"

"Exactly."

"Or...hmm," I think about other horror movies, "hubris."

"Gee whiz, what big words you use."

I laugh.

"Alright, induct me," I say.

Ginny pulls up a movie, a black and white film. "Prepare to have your pants scared off," she says.

Hmm, I kind of like that thought.

I try my best not to look at her skirt inching its way up her legs. The movie starts. Ginny relaxes back into the couch, but I can't relax. I'm hyperaware of her. I notice every time she shifts, or catches her breath, or leans forward in excitement. My body tingles and I just want to inch closer to her. I can't pay attention to the movie when she's right there next to me. It's getting scarier though, I can tell because her breath comes faster and she's all tense.

I ache to touch her. What would a friend do? A friend could hold her hand if she were scared, couldn't he?

I drop my hand to the couch, palm up and rest it close to her. I don't look at her, I just let it rest there. She glances down at it then up at me. I don't say anything and neither does she. After a minute of neither of us moving or saying anything at all, she nestles her hand into mine. I let out the breath I was holding. I have no idea what happens for the rest of the movie, the only thing I can see or feel is the weight of her hand resting in mine. The touch of her, the heat, the warm vibration traveling up my arm and through the rest of my body. Every breath I take I have to restrain myself from taking her hand and pulling her to me.

The movie ends and the credits roll over the screen. Neither of us moves. We sit there, still as stone, her hand nestled in mine. The credits stop. The screen goes blank and the music ends. Still, we don't move.

Finally, she pulls her hand out of mine.

"Did you like it?" she whispers.

I swallow. "It was incredible."

"I thought you might," she says. "That was one of the original..."

I turn to her and she trails off. Her lips twitch and she licks them. Then, "One of the precursors to..."

"To?"

She shakes her head and her eyes are glassy. "Don't remember."

"Right."

She leans forward and runs her fingers along my jawbone. They're light on my skin and send a shock through me. I look into her eyes. She doesn't look away as her hand sends shivers across me. Finally, she drops her hand to her lap.

"See you in the morning," she whispers.

I curl my fingers in the couch cushion so that I don't reach out and pull her to me.

"Sure thing," I say. With extreme difficulty I give her a devil may care smile.

"We should do this again sometime," she says. She walks me to the door.

I nod, and suddenly I feel like a sixteen-year-old standing at the door of his first date. Kiss her, don't kiss her, kiss her, don't—

"It's good having a friend," she says.

Right. Don't kiss her.

"Sure is."

Her eyes are tired, but happy. That's alright then.

"Goodnight, Ginny."

Goodnight, friend.

14

Ginny

*T*he late nights where Liam and I hang out have become routine. He works out in the morning, then I go to work or take Bean to her appointments, then we come back together in the evening for superhero training with Bean if she's not too tired. It sort of became an unspoken agreement that Liam would stick around while I tuck Bean into bed and then we just hang out.

"I can't believe you never learned how to do a cartwheel," I say.

"I'm a guy," he says. He crosses his arms over his chest and gives me a look like I should know better than to think a guy would do a cartwheel.

"Yeah, so. It's secret or stunt. You either have to tell me a secret or do a stunt."

He looks at the living room. There's definitely not enough room in here for him to attempt a cartwheel.

He sighs and shakes his head at me.

I grin evilly.

"Fine. I hate lima beans. Can't eat them, they're like disgusting beany turtles. They make me gag."

I start to laugh, then stop when I see that he's serious. "You're kidding."

"No, I'm not kidding. Your turn."

"But that's not a secret."

"Sure it is. Nobody else knows it. Just you and me."

"Huh."

I tuck my legs under me and lean back into the couch. I came up with the game this afternoon. Liam took Bean to a gymnastics open gym. She couldn't do too many of the activities, but she still loved it. I guess I got into the spirit. I suggested the game after I tucked her in.

Liam considers me for a moment and I shift under his scrutiny. There's a slight indentation in his chin and I have the strongest urge to lick it. His eyes narrow on me, like he can hear my thoughts.

"What's the stunt?" I ask, trying to distract him.

"A backwards somersault," he says.

I grin at him. I could do a backwards somersault in my sleep.

"Tell me a secret," he says as he looks at my lips. "Or do a backwards somersault."

I pull my gaze away from his chin and look up at him. "I want you to come to the end of summer picnic with us."

"That's your secret?"

"Oh. No, I mean...it just popped into my head." I pull my lip through my teeth. "It's a yearly thing. Enid invites the neighborhood, we grill out in the backyard, have games."

"Alright," he says. "Sounds fun."

Because he'd be there as a friend. I look at his hands. They're both on the couch, palm down. He's not inviting me to hold them. He hasn't.

"Hmm. A secret," I say. I can't think of any, I'm too focused on the trace of stubble over his jaw and his lip. "Nope," I say. Then I stand up and perform a backwards somersault. "Ta-da," I say as I pop back up.

"Chicken," he says.

I drop back onto the couch and sink closer to him.

"I'll tell another. I'm not afraid."

"Oh really?"

He nods. "When I was a kid, I wanted to be a doctor."

"You did?" I'm surprised, that's so far from where he ended up.

"Yeah. Then I realized how long I'd have to be in school and I changed my mind."

"You didn't like school?"

"I liked recess."

"Ridiculous."

He grins at me and flashes the dimple in his cheek. "I mean, I liked being able to make kids laugh."

"You were the class clown?"

"Oh yeah."

"Let me guess. You wanted to be the center of attention."

He frowns and looks up. "Kind of. I was a really shy kid."

"Really?"

He nods. "I learned pretty quickly that if I could make kids laugh, or act goofy, that I'd have friends. And no one would notice that I wasn't talking or approaching people any other time. Nobody notices you're terrified of talking to people if you're joking or acting funny."

Huh. I guess that's true. I never thought about it before. "Are you still shy?"

"Not anymore."

"You don't have trouble talking, or saying what you want."

"Not usually," he says. He eyes flick again to my lips and they start to tingle from the attention.

"I'm taking classes online, for my degree," I say. "It's a secret."

"Why?" he asks.

I shrug. "It feels weird doing something for myself. And I think if people knew, and I didn't finish, I'd feel like a bigger failure than if I was the only one that knew about it."

"Why?"

"Because. The time I'm spending studying could go to working more or to spending time with Bean. Or the money I spend on tuition, that could go to getting an apartment or better clothes or more groceries or medical bills."

"Hey," he says. I'm working myself up and he puts a finger to my cheek, then tucks a strand of hair behind my ear.

"What?" I ask, kind of scared at what he's going to say.

"You're doing good."

I tighten up at the words.

"You're doing good," he repeats.

"One more secret," I say.

He nods.

"It's hard being a caregiver. You stop taking care of yourself. You stop being anything but a caregiver. And you keep giving. And giving. Sometimes, it seems like there won't be anything left and I'll lose myself in the process." There's a hard pinch in my chest. "But then, I feel so selfish even thinking that."

He doesn't say anything and I feel like he must be judging me. I'm scared to look at his face, but I make myself look up.

I sort of crumble when I do see his expression. Because there's no judgment, just understanding.

"Thanks," I say. I let out a long sigh.

"I think you should keep pursuing your degree," he says.

"I will." I hold up three fingers. "Scout's honor."

"I'll go with you to the picnic," he says.

"Oh," I say. I'd forgotten I asked him. "Thank you."

15

Liam

I'm at the picnic and Enid has cornered me at the dessert table.

"Enjoying yourself?" she asks.

I look at her face and see if I'm hearing her sarcasm correctly, but I can't make out her expression under the brim of her sun hat.

"I am. Thank you, ma'am," I say.

"Don't thank me. I didn't invite you." It's pretty clear that she wouldn't have invited me if she'd been asked for input.

"Ah. Well..." I go to pick up a slice of apple pie for Ginny and a piece of carrot cake for Bean, but Enid holds out her hand over the desserts. I stop and turn back to her.

"You're not a drunk."

"No, ma'am."

The wrinkles on her face deepen. "Beatrice likes you," she says, and her mouth turns down like she tastes something awful.

I'm not sure who she's talking about at first, then I remember that she calls Bean Beatrice.

"She's a good kid," I say.

"I wish you'd never come around," she says. "I wish you'd stayed in that trailer and pickled yourself to death."

I drop my chin to my chest and stare in shock at the woman. I knew she didn't like me, but this takes all.

"All due respect—"

"I have some advice. Because I care about my daughter-in-law and granddaughter."

I stop. I look at Ginny off on the other side of the yard, she and Bean are playing cards on a picnic blanket, but she's looking over at me and her forehead wrinkles. Yeah, she's concerned about this conversation.

"Okay," I say.

Enid turns and scoops a piece of lemon meringue pie onto a paper plate.

"They don't need you complicating their life."

I go to reply but she stops me.

"They don't need a friend, they don't need a superhero. They need a miracle. And unless you can give them a miracle, I suggest you get out of their lives before you do them damage."

"I..." I don't know what to say.

She takes in my expression and nods. "That's what I thought," she says bitterly. "Try the lemon meringue. It's not too sour."

She walks away, back toward Finick and a group of his friends. She starts to terrorize them when she realizes they're throwing pocket knives at the walnut tree.

I finish scooping desserts onto the plate. I choose randomly, not able to concentrate on the task anymore. She's right. They don't need me, they need a miracle.

Bean needs a donor, and so far, they haven't found one in all the donor registries in the whole wide world. She's running out of time.

On my way back to the picnic blanket, Heather steps in my path.

"You're looking good, Stoney," she says.

"Thanks," I say in a curt voice. I'm not in the mood.

"Having fun with Ginny and little Bean?" she asks. The way she asks the question makes it clear she doubts it.

"Yes. Very much." I try to move past her but she grabs my wrist. I stop, the plate of desserts balanced between us.

"I heard you're headed back to Hollywood. Another big role on the horizon," she says.

"Heard more than me then," I say. I still haven't heard anything from my agent after I turned down the hemorrhoid commercial. Although, the thought of that commercial sparks something in the back of my mind. A little flicker of an idea.

I look down at her hand on my wrist and then back up at her. I bring back the glare that used to terrify assistants.

She drops her hand and steps back quickly. Her expression changes from coy to angry.

"I just wanted to give you a friendly warning," she says. "But I guess it wouldn't be appreciated."

"No," I say. The place between my shoulder blades itches.

"Well. Far be it from me to tell you what you should already know."

"What's that?" I ask, hoping that the sooner she spits it out the sooner I can get back to Ginny and Bean.

"Ginny's using you. She expects you to be the Prince Charming to her Cinderella. She plays the role of desperate maiden so well that before you know it you'll be shackled and living in Centreville the rest of your life. In your trailer. Or a garage. If it were up to her, you'd never get back to Hollywood. I've seen it happen before. She derails men."

I look at Heather and all I see is hate, and one other thing that I'm certain of, "We were never in a movie together."

Her face goes white then she composes herself. "Of course we were. I was an extra. I worked on lots of sets as an extra."

I shake my head. "I don't think so."

She glares at me and the color floods back into her face. Before she can say anything I gesture to Finick. He's got his knife out again and is flinging it at the tree. "Your son's getting into trouble."

Her mouth opens wide and she goes white again. "He's... he's not my..." She hurries away, toward Finick. Right, he's her brother.

I sigh and shake it off.

Between Enid and Heather, I've had enough confrontations to last a year.

I sit on the blanket and set the dessert plate down.

"There you go," I say. "Enough sugar to keep you awake for a week."

"Yay," says Bean. She takes a big bite of the carrot cake.

"You alright?" asks Ginny. "I saw you talking, it looked kind of heated."

"It's fine," I say. "They just wanted to say how much they admire my movies."

Ginny gives me a disbelieving look, then, "You're so full of it."

I grin. "You got that right."

The bad feeling I had after talking with Enid and Heather lifts. I spend the rest of the afternoon eating insane amounts of hot dogs, corn on the cob, watermelon and pie. We play cards and horseshoes and lay in the sun. At dusk, Bean tries to coax fireflies to land on her hand. I grab one from the sky and hold it out on my palm. Bean's face lights up when the firefly glows for her. She reaches out her finger and it climbs on.

"Mama, Mama. You see that? I've got a lightning bug on my

finger." Bean laughs as it flashes bright yellow. "It tickles," she says.

"That's amazing," Ginny says.

She looks over at me and her eyes are filled with so much happiness that my heart stops then starts again with a hard thud.

Just friends. We're just friends. I'm just helping out, then heading back to Hollywood.

Enid's words play back in my mind. They need a miracle, not a friend.

The firefly lights up again and Bean laughs as it flies up into the sky. It joins the others and they fill the gray dusk with twinkling yellow light.

"I'm so happy," says Bean.

"Me too, baby," says Ginny. She pulls Bean into her lap and they lean back to watch the fireflies.

I look up at the sky. The fireflies blink in then out. Then I look at Ginny and Bean. I rub my chest, and it aches under my hand. They need a miracle.

Ginny is anything but a damsel in distress. She can do whatever she puts her mind to, she can even be her own hero. But can she find a miracle?

I don't know.

16

Ginny

The summer's nearly gone. It's been six weeks since I met Liam. I brush my hand across Bean's head and drop a kiss on her cheek. It's early, before sunrise. Bean snuggles in her bed, the big teddy from the county fair, christened Pinky, is in her arms, and she's sound asleep. I slip through the adjoining door into the kitchen of the house. Enid stands at the stove flipping pancakes.

"She's still asleep," I say.

Enid's shoulders stiffen, but she doesn't say anything. The longer we've been seeing Liam, the less she's said anything, but if anything, her disapproval has gotten stronger.

"I'll be back by eight."

She turns and points her spatula at me. "You're getting too attached."

I step back from the spatula. "What?"

"All Bean talks about is Liam Stone this, Liam Stone that. You don't talk about him, but I can tell you think about him.

You spend every night together, afternoons, and evenings, too. He came to the *picnic*."

"Yes?" She's right, we have spent nearly every day of the past six weeks together. Except the days we're at the children's hospital, or the days I have a long shift at work. Bean's so happy, and I've been…happy too. "You make it sound like a crime."

"It is," she snaps. She turns and flips the pancakes.

"I know you believe—"

She turns again and waves the spatula at me. "I was wrong. That man's not a bad seed, and he's fit for decent company."

"Okay?" This is unexpected.

"He's even worse. He's a fine man, and because you're vulnerable, you're getting too attached. That man's set on leaving, and when he does you're in for a mountain of misery. You and Bean both." Her eyes are watery and her mouth drawn down. She's speaking from experience. My heart reaches out to her, and although she's never welcomed it, I want to hug her.

"I miss him too," I whisper. She knows who I'm talking about. He's the only person we both miss.

The lines around her mouth deepen and she turns back to the stove. She flips the cooked pancakes onto the plate next to the griddle. They hit the plate with a forlorn plop. When she's done she places her hands on the counter.

"Do what you'll do," she says. "But don't say I didn't warn you."

She doesn't turn back around. Her back's so straight that I know she's keeping herself together by sheer will. I shouldn't have said it. We don't talk about George. His death is a ghost here, even though Enid removed every bit of him, scrubbed the house clean of his memory, he still comes in. A song will play on the TV, and by her reaction, I can tell it reminds her of him. Or, sometimes when Bean laughs, she has to leave the room. Their laugh is the same. It's like bells ringing on a clear, spring day. I love it. But Enid…

"I'm sorry."

Her shoulders stiffen, but she doesn't take her hands off the counter, or turn, or acknowledge me.

It's always seemed to me that the way Enid dealt with her son's death was trying to forget he ever existed. But maybe I've been wrong. Maybe the pain is just too big for her, even now. She's trying to protect herself. Maybe instead of the heart of stone I imagined, it's a heart too soft.

"Thank you for being worried for us."

I wait a moment for her answer, but she doesn't say anything. Grandpa Clark comes into the kitchen, a Vietnam War modeling magazine in his hand.

"You're still here?" he asks in surprise.

Enid stands up straight and starts pouring more pancake batter.

"Just leaving. I'll be back by eight. Bean's still sleeping."

"Alright, bye then."

I jog to the car. I'm a few minutes late. Liam will be waiting.

~

"Tell me about your husband," says Liam a few days later.

I look at him in surprise, but he's doing pushups, so I can't see his face.

"Why?" I ask.

"You never talk about him. Bean doesn't talk about him except to say he was a hero."

"Bean never met him," I say.

"Why not?"

Liam flips on one hand and does a perfect side plank. He doesn't need me anymore. It's pretty clear that there's not any reason for him to stick around. He's cut, lean, and in silver screen shape. He could jump into filming tomorrow. Enid was right, he'll be leaving soon.

He drops back down and starts on another set of pushups.

"I was only in early pregnancy when he died." I look around the field, at the trees at the trailer, and think about how unexpected life is. In that car, seven years ago, I never would've thought I'd be standing here.

"Ah, so she just has stories of him."

I nod, even though Liam can't see it. "I tell her the funny stories. Like how he could do any accent perfectly, and he'd get us into the most ridiculous situations. And I tell her the romantic stories, like how we met and right away I knew I was going to marry him. He came up to me and said, 'Hey, pretty lady, I think you stole my heart.' Then he smiled and I was a goner. So I tell her the story of how we met and then about how he died. How she and I wouldn't be here if it weren't for him. How he loved her so much that he gave his life so she could live. That he didn't think anything of going back for her and saving her life. Even though he'd never met her. He loved her that much. That's what I tell her. That he loved her so much."

"I'm sure he did," says Liam. He pushes up from the ground and stands next to me. "Sorry, you don't have to talk about it."

I wipe at my eye and shake my head. "No, it's alright. I don't mind it."

"Sort of a hard act to follow, isn't it?"

"Yeah. I did set the bar impossibly high," I say. I can't really live up to the image I painted in my stories, and neither, maybe, can anyone else. "Maybe I should tell Bean a few stories that show her dad as a person. The good along with the bad."

It's the flaws that make us beautiful after all.

"Don't know," he says. "Life's complicated."

Liam smiles and stretches out his arms and shoulders. Then, without needing to say anything, we start jogging down the trail. He turns down the fork and heads toward the stream.

When we get there he stops and starts to kick off his shoes and socks.

"Come on," he says. "I've been wanting to do this for weeks."

I smile as I watch him test the water with his bare feet.

"That's cold," he says.

But he settles down and dunks his feet in the clear running water. He pats the ground next to him.

"Alright, alright," I say. We have a good forty-five minutes before I need to get back. I pull off my shoes and socks and settle on the mossy ground next to him. I dip my feet into the water. It's cold as ice and feels amazing.

Liam leans back on his elbows and I lean back too. We're quiet for a minute. The spongy moss beneath us, the birds calling each other from the tree branches, the sound of the stream running swiftly by. I pull my feet out of the water before they go numb.

"You're leaving soon, aren't you?" I ask. We've talked about nearly everything, except this. I guess I thought that if I ignored it, it wouldn't happen.

He plays with the springy moss, pressing it up and down. Then he looks up at me.

"We're friends, yeah?" he asks.

I'm startled by his question.

"Of course we're friends," I say. After watching the movie, we've been nothing but friends. Talking, hanging out, training, going on adventures with Bean. I've even shared with him my dreams about starting my own wellness center. I've not shared that with anyone. One night, I told him how scared I am. Of everything. I've told him more than I've told anyone in my whole life. No one knows me better. No one. We're friends. But more.

There hasn't been any more holding hands since that first

night. And there haven't been any more kisses. He's been just a friend. The best friend I could've ever imagined.

God, I'm going to miss him.

"My agent called," he says.

I look over at him and a cold dread washes over me. This is it then.

"What did he say?" I ask.

"I haven't called him back yet," he says. He throws a flower head into the stream and it's carried away on the current.

"But you will," I say.

He nods.

Suddenly, I want to tell him not to call his agent back. Not to go. That he doesn't have to go. He can stay here and we can keep on like this forever. But even as I think it, I know it's the wrong thing to do. He wouldn't be happy here. His place is in Hollywood. He's told me the stories, how much he loved it, how being an actor is a part of him. I look over at him. There's not a trace of the man I met that first day in the trailer. Then, he was hungover, out of shape, and, what did I call him...a villain?

Now, he stands tall, he laughs, he has so much energy and life. He's filled with so much anticipation. For his future.

Not for staying in Centreville, Ohio with a widow and her daughter.

Plus, even if he asked, I couldn't uproot Bean. She has her grandma and grandpa. She has the doctors and nurses she trusts at the children's hospital. And then after everything. I think of Enid, her mountains of misery and her years of pain. I don't know who I'll become...after. So, this little bit of time, this is it.

"I think," I say on a rush of feeling, "you're the best person I've ever known."

He looks over at me quickly. "Don't say that."

"You are."

"Just because I'm leaving soon, don't get all nostalgic on me.

Pretty soon you'll only be telling the good stories about me. Leaving out all the bad."

"Come on."

"Don't make me a hero," he says.

I roll my eyes. "You're a superhero."

"You know what I mean."

I do.

"How about I tell you some bad stories about me?"

I smile and shift closer to him. Then because the moss is spongy and I'm starting to relax I lay my head on his shoulder. He stiffens then lets out a breath and wraps his arm around me. It feels so good to be held.

"Tell me," I say.

"I was a class-A jerk in Hollywood."

"You were not," I say.

"Oh yeah. A-hole with a capital A."

"No, come on. I don't believe it."

"I had two personal assistants. Every morning, they had to bring me a triple espresso cappuccino. If it wasn't exactly 140 degrees with two inches of foam I sent them back for another. One day, I sent it back four times."

I start to laugh. "You *were* an a-hole."

He grimaces. "Yeah. It sounds moronic. But that's what I was like then. During filming, I had requirements. A bowl of *only* yellow M&M's. A specific brand of bottled water. I wouldn't talk to any actor below hot shot status. If a staff member annoyed me, I fired them. I didn't care about people."

"You sound...awesome."

"I was an ass."

I lean in and rest my arm over his chest. He's warm and I like the feel of him. I splay my fingers over his heart and rub a little circle with my pointer finger.

"I thought, being one of the highest-paid actors in Hollywood, that I had a right to walk all over people. If anyone called me on it, which they rarely did, I thought they were jealous, or had an attitude. It never occurred to me that they could be right. I was making millions, and they were fetching coffee, or working minimum wage, what could they know?"

I run my hand up his collarbone and along the tendons in his neck. He cut his hair, but the ends still curl at the base of his neck. For weeks I've been wanting to feel it. So I let myself. It's as soft and silky as I imagined. He lies still beneath me. He's so powerful, so solid. It's hard to picture him as the person he's describing.

"But you were such a *good* person in your movies."

"It was an act. I was acting."

"Were you? I mean—"

"I was. Trust me, I wasn't a nice guy."

"And then..."

"I fell."

"Broke your back and your hip."

"And all those people in Hollywood that I'd treated like crap—"

"They were happy to see you go?"

"No. My assistants, the woman that filled the coffee in the break room, the guy that got the flipping M&M's, they were the only ones to visit me while I was in the hospital. The people that I'd dismissed as not worthwhile were the only ones to show a speck of humanity. I found out pretty quickly that I wasn't as irreplaceable as I'd believed. Just as quickly as I'd dropped the faulty assistants, Hollywood dropped me."

"I'm sorry."

He runs a hand over my back, and I stretch into his touch.

"I'm not."

I look up at his face in surprise. "Why not?"

"In Bean's words," he says, "breaking my back was my origin story. It transformed me from Grade A a-hole to who I am now."

"A little wiser," I say.

"A little nicer."

"A little uglier."

He jerks under me. "Hey."

"And bad at pushups." I say.

He laughs and then flips me under him. His arms cage me in and his legs rest alongside my own.

"You think so?" he asks.

"I know so. I'm your trainer." I smirk up at him. There's a happiness low in my belly, but also a growing warmth. I want to pull him down or tilt up my hips to meet him. We've not touched this last month, but oh how I've wanted to.

"How's this?" he asks. He drops his arms down and does a pushup over me. His nose touches mine and then he pushes back up. He hovers just above me.

"Weak," I say. I hold back a smile.

"And this?" he asks. He pushes down again and then up.

"Try again."

He does. He drops down then up, down then up, until he's moving in a rhythm over me. Is this what it would be like to be with him? When he moves down, his body brushes mine. Our hips meet, our noses touch, and his lips are just a whisper away.

"And now?" he asks.

"Keep trying," I say. My voice sounds throatier than usual.

When he hears the huskiness his pupils dilate. He lowers more slowly onto me and I hold myself back from tilting up to meet him. My breasts feel heavy and I'm starting to ache. I want to rock into him.

"And this?" he asks. His mouth is so close. I could tilt my chin up and we'd meet.

I shake my head no.

He smiles and pushes up again. His hip bones graze against me and I hold back a moan.

"Now?"

"More," I say.

He smiles and lowers down again. Finally, he lets our whole bodies meet. His chest presses into my breasts and sends tingles across my nipples. His hips press into mine and I feel the long, thick length of him. Warmth bursts through me and I rock up into him.

"Yeah?" he asks.

"Yes."

His lips tangle over mine and he rubs them across. He lifts himself up and watches my face. His eyes flare when he sees my expression. Then he lowers back down. I let out a long exhale as he comes back to me.

"Better," I say.

He rests down on his forearms and tilts his head to mine.

"Can I kiss you?"

I drop my eyelids until I'm looking at him through a haze.

"Please."

With aching slowness he lowers his lips to mine. When he does it's like a star bursts to life inside me. The whole world is consumed with brightness and the birth of something beautiful. I gasp and he captures my mouth. Presses himself into me and I cry out as he rubs his length over me. His tongue tangles with mine and I feel like we're trading secrets. For a month we've been talking, learning each other, sharing everything. Now, we're just doing it in another way. He's telling me that he cares for me, that he wants me, needs me. I'm telling him that I'll miss him, that he's the best man I've ever known, that I need him too.

I taste him and he tastes like kindness and goodness.

Then, I stop tasting, stop thinking and just feel.

He keeps up the rhythm of the pushups, but instead of leaving me, he drives his length over me. He drags it across my shorts and I push back up to him. It runs against my clit and sends sparks over me that grow and grow. I ache for him. I grab his back with my hands and pull him close. I want him closer.

He runs his lips over my mouth. His kiss is deep and intimate, and his mouth works in concert with his hips. I wrap my legs around him and he groans into my mouth. The deep rumble of it spreads a vibration through me all the way down my legs.

He rubs harder along me and I cry out at the burst of pleasure. He catches my cry in his mouth.

I want him. I want him so much.

"Please," I say.

I want to be in charge of this moment. But he still has me trapped under him.

He pushes harder against me and I forget what I was thinking. There's only him and me, rocking our hips together, pressing our lips together. The rhythm grows faster. The pressure builds and builds, until I'm clawing at his back and I can't stand it anymore.

White starbursts flash in my eyes and I cry out. My hips buck up against him and I hold onto him as I ride out the orgasm ripping through me. He takes my cries and kisses my lips. His hands tug at my hair and tilt my chin up so that he can kiss me more and more. Finally, the pressure subsides and the tension and the release leave, until all I can do is collapse back to the ground. Liam lifts his lips from mine and runs his fingers through my hair.

He looks down at me with a dazed expression. I'm still caught under him. He just watches me, doesn't say anything at all.

But he doesn't need to. I can read him.

"Thank you," I say.

He leans down and presses a long lingering kiss to my lips.

"I'll miss you," I say.

"I'm not gone yet," he says.

And we kiss again. This time, the secret I tell him, the one with my mouth and my kiss, is that I love him, I love him and I only just realized it. But I'm not going to keep him here, and I'm not going to keep him from his dreams. But all the same, I love him so much.

I suppose that's where the mountain of misery comes in. But right now, it feels so good.

17

Liam

I leave Centreville for a week. After I called my agent back we talked over the idea I had at the picnic. He booked the commercial and got me on location to film in record time. Ginny and I didn't talk about what happened by the stream. Hell, I'm not exactly sure what happened, or more importantly, where to go from here. The lines are no longer clear. We're not just friends, we're more, but not...I don't know. I don't know how to define the role I play in her life.

I know what role they play in mine. She and Bean are the reason I'm here. They've both lodged themselves in my heart so deep that I'll never be able to get them out.

I took the week of filming to get perspective. To see if being away made my feelings change. But they didn't. If anything, they grew stronger. I'm going to ask Ginny for more. To be more than friends. I know I've said I'm leaving Centreville, and by my agent's response, and the interest from the studios, I'll be getting some calls soon. But...I don't want to leave Ginny and

Bean. We could make it work. Plenty of people have long-distance relationships.

I didn't let Ginny know that I'm back in town. I head straight to her place, and when she answers her door she looks a little tired and a lot sad. But then she sees it's me and her face lights up.

"You're back," she says.

"I'm back," I say. And suddenly I feel like that awkward teenager again. Kiss her, don't kiss her, kiss her.

"Liam," shouts Bean.

Don't kiss her.

Bean runs to me and puts her arms around my waist. "You came back. Grandma said you wouldn't. She said you're a mountain of misery. And Heather said you should stay in Hollywood because Mama is a man-eater and then Finick said Heather was a bitter cow and Joel said that Finick should be glad his sister took him in and Finick said he wishes she hadn't and then—"

"I'm glad to see you too." I say.

Bean pulls out of the hug and says, "Well, I believed in you. And so did Mama. But no one else did." She says this solemnly with a great deal of meaning. Seems like they're the only ones who always believe in me. The knowledge that I'm doing the right thing settles in my chest. This past week away, filming the commercial was the right thing to do.

"I've got a surprise," I say. "A superhero training."

Ginny raises her eyebrows. "Really? Today?"

I nod.

I can tell that Ginny's holding back a whole lot of questions about the past week. We talked on the phone, and texted, but not enough, and not about what happened by the stream.

"Am I finally gonna learn to fly?" asks Bean. She looks more tired too, and a little more pale than usual. Even her hug was a bit subdued. Maybe this surprise will help buck her up.

"Am I finally, finally gonna get to fly?"

I rub her head. "You better believe it."

Bean squeals and the look on Ginny's face is priceless.

"I'm gonna fly, I'm gonna fly," shouts Bean, and she spins in a circle with her arms wide.

I share a smile with Ginny at Bean's enthusiasm.

Then I step closer to Ginny and gently set the back of my hand against hers. She looks at me, but doesn't pull away.

"I missed you," I say. Which feels a lot like putting myself out on a ledge. Ginny doesn't say anything right away and I wonder if she's going to let me fall off the ledge and not say anything at all.

But after a moment she says quietly, "I missed you too."

The tension I was holding releases.

It'll be alright.

When we get to the private airport Bean is nearly floating she's so excited.

We get a tour of the small airport and Bean gets to see the different vehicles. Then the pilot takes us to a four-seater Cessna. The wings sit high above the cockpit so we're going to have a great view of the ground.

"It's called the Skyhawk," the pilot says. She's retired Air Force and teaches flying now.

"Wow," says Bean. "The Skyhawk." Her eyes are huge and she asks a thousand questions a minute. We climb up and the pilot shows Bean all the controls.

Then Bean settles down in the co-pilot seat, and Ginny and I sit in the back. We put on our headsets and get all set to go.

"I'm gonna fly," Bean says, and the way she says it makes me want to buy her an airplane. The darn kid, she has no idea the effect she has.

"You sure are," I say.

Ginny reaches over and places her hand in mine. "Thank you," she mouths.

"Of course," I say. How could I not? Bean's been wanting to fly from the moment I met her.

The plane starts down the runway and my stomach dips as we lift into the air. Bean squeals as the wheels leave the ground. Then she points out all the landmarks that she knows: the school, the grocery store, the playground, the library. When Bean sees the wooded park near my place and points out the trail, Ginny blushes. I run my thumb over the back of Ginny's hand and she looks at me from under her eyelashes.

"There's our house," says Bean. "There it is. Hi Grandma, hi Grandpa." She waves madly and is convinced they can see her and are waving back.

Ginny grins at me and all the tiredness that I saw when I got back just melts away. We're not talking, but I can tell what she's thinking, because I'm thinking it too. We've left it all behind. The complications, the worry, the future. None of that matters right now. When the plane left the ground, we dropped all that and right now, we're free.

I run my fingers over Ginny's hand, her palm, then I lace my fingers through hers. She watches the bluish-green hills, the blur of trees, the red painted barns, and I watch her.

As Bean laughs in the pilot seat and Ginny smiles at me with that look in her eyes, I feel, no believe, that we can do anything. There isn't anything in the future that we can't handle. Together.

Ginny takes in my look and quirks an eyebrow in question. I wink at her.

This is it. We're going to be okay.

When the plane comes down and the tires hit the ground I still feel that sense of rightness.

"That was awesome," says Bean as she's lifted down from the plane. "I flew. I really flew."

"You sure did," I say. "Looks like you're a certified sidekick now."

Her eyes go wide and she says, "Wo-ow. Mama, did you hear? I'm a sidekick. A real sidekick."

"That's amazing, baby," says Ginny. She takes Bean from me and hugs her tight into her chest. "You did it." She kisses the top of Bean's head, and when Ginny looks up her eyes are misty. "I'm so happy for you."

"You'll need a name," I say.

"Skyhawk," says Bean.

It's settled. The only other thing she needs is her very own superhero outfit.

"I'm the happiest I've been in my whole life," she says.

Ginny squeezes her tight. "Me too."

18

Ginny

*L*iam and I lie in the grass in his yard and look up at the stars. The sky is inky black and clear. The moon is a small crescent and the stars shine brilliant white. It looks like there are thousands of them tonight.

"Are the stars the same in California?" I ask. The sound of crickets picks up, crescendos then quiets down again.

"In LA? No." I wonder if he looked at the sky when he was there last week.

"Why not?"

"You can't see them. Not like this. Ursa Major." He points up at the constellation. "Ursa Minor. Cepheus. Cassiopeia. Draco."

I smile and try to make out where he points. "How do you know the constellations?"

"Liam Stone's an astronomer. I learned them for the role."

"Right. I forgot." His superhero character was an astronomer before he gained his cosmic powers through a galactic accident. "I just figured you picked it up to impress dates."

"Is that what this is?" he asks. He rolls over and looks down at me.

Heat spreads across my face. "No," I say, then I look away, because it does feel like a date.

After the plane ride I tucked Bean in and then asked Enid if she could watch her for a few hours. Liam drove me out to his place for some quiet. We ended up here, lying on the ground, looking at the stars.

"That's too bad," he says. He looks at my mouth and a low hum spreads through me.

"Thank you again. For what you did today."

"Of course. I wanted to."

I turn back to look up at him. "But you didn't have to. You've done so much, and you didn't have to do any of it. When you left this week..." I trail off, not certain I can admit it.

"Hey," he says. He runs his finger along my cheek. "Okay?"

"Yeah." I swallow and say what I'm afraid to. "When you left I realized how much I've come to depend on you." My heart thuds and I swallow back the fear.

"That's okay," he says.

"Is it?" I whisper.

He nods. "It's okay to depend on me."

I shake my head. Before he came, I was doing okay. Well, not okay, but...it worked. Now, I got a taste of what it's going to be like when he leaves. It wasn't pretty. It hurt. Missing him hurt.

"How?" I ask.

"You have to trust," he says.

I look up at him. He smiles and his eyes are clear and earnest. I'm lying back, the smell of lush grass and nighttime surround me, crickets sing, and the stars shine above. The sounds fade and this feels like a moment where I can step forward or pull back. And I don't think I can step forward, there's too much I'm afraid of.

"I should go," I say. "Get back to Bean."

"Enid has her. She's sound asleep. You should stay."

I want to. I want to stay, but for so long I've thought first of Bean that it feels wrong to think of myself. Because to admit that I want Liam for myself, at least for one night, seems selfish.

He watches my face and I think he sees the doubt in my expression.

"Hey. Don't go," he says.

"Go where?"

"Wherever it is when you look like that. You pull away. You look tired and sad and I don't like it."

So he can see it. All the fatigue and worry I try so hard to hide.

Maybe I can depend on him. Maybe for one night, I can be with him. I can do something without thinking about what might come tomorrow or the next day. I can just be.

He senses the moment I make the decision.

"You'll stay?" he asks.

"If I asked," I whisper. He leans forward to hear me better. "If I asked, could I depend on you..."

"Yes."

"To kiss me?"

I hold my breath as he looks down at me. Then a smile spreads over his face, his smile, not the fake Liam Stone smile, but his smile. I exhale.

"Hell yeah, you can."

Then he sinks down on top of me. He puts his knees between my thighs and pushes them apart so that they form a cradle for him to sink into. He lays on top of me and I send my ankles down his back and his thighs. He props on his forearms and puts his forehead to mine.

"Okay?" he asks.

"Shut up and kiss me."

His eyes crinkle and he laughs. As he does I reach up and capture his mouth. His surprise doesn't last long. He pushes me down and works his mouth over mine. He draws his lips over me and starts the rhythm of where we left off last week. He takes my lower lip in his and draws on it until I moan.

He pulls away. "I'm going to kiss you," he says.

I run my hands through his hair and pull him back to me. I lick his mouth and taste him. He tastes familiar and sweet. His hand brushes over my ribcage and I lift up at the electricity of his touch. He cups my breast and my nipples ache to be touched. He pinches it between his fingers and I gasp at the sensation. He pinches my nipple again and there's an echoing pulse between my thighs. I lift up to him and feel his hardness.

He moans and pushes away from me.

"Let me," he says.

"What?"

"Kiss you."

His hips rock against mine and I see exactly what he means. "Yes," I say.

His eyes light with triumph. He sits back on his knees between my legs. My hair splays out on the ground and I feel warm and wanton. My lips are kiss-swollen and my body aches with need.

Liam draws his hands over my ribs and down to my thighs. He flicks the buttons loose and then he slowly draws down my jeans. They scrape against my thighs and calves and I feel heightened to every touch. When he sees my pink lace panties he sucks in a sharp breath.

I give him a smile and he watches my expression as he slowly tugs them down. When I'm bare to him he spreads his hands over my hips and dips his head. At the whisper of his breath over me I lift my hips and cry out. His fingers dig into my side and his mouth brushes over me. Then he starts to *kiss*.

Except it's more like a dance. His mouth twirls around me, pulls me in, then lets me go, only to pull me in again. Soon, I can't tell whether my eyes are opened or closed, or whether it's me yelling or him. I grab at the grass and lift my hips in the air. It's building and I don't want him to stop.

"Please don't stop. Don't stop."

He rumbles something against me, and everything unleashes. I spiral and he kisses me and holds me and then I can't...

"I can't..."

"You can."

He takes me in his mouth again and his fingers press into me and I ride his mouth and the sweetness that he's giving me. Finally, finally, I fall back to the earth. I'm out of breath, a little lightheaded, and my heart pounds. My body feels delicious. Then, Liam looks up at me and his eyes light with smug satisfaction. He grins at me and I hold open my arms.

"Come here."

He raises up to me and I tug at his pants. In seconds he's flung them off and we both pull off our shirts, I unsnap my bra and for a moment the frenzy to undress pauses as he takes in my breasts.

"My word," he says. He takes me in, naked beneath him. "Reality is a million times better than fantasy."

"You fantasized?"

"Since the day I met you," he says.

"Liar."

"It's true. I always wanted you, even if I didn't want to admit it."

I smile at him. It's hard to look anywhere but his eyes, especially when he's looking at me like he is, but I glance down. He's back to the old Liam, the superhero physique, except, there's something different, and I think it's the way he looks at me. That's something no one has ever seen. And it's just for me.

"I want you," I say, and it's not hard to admit.

"I want you too."

He leans down and brushes a kiss over my mouth.

I close my eyes and he presses a kiss on each eyelid.

"You want this?" he asks.

I swallow and nod, then, "I do."

He smiles down at me then takes my mouth in his. I pull my hands over his shoulders and raise my hips to meet him. He settles between my legs and sets himself at my entrance. As we kiss, he rocks himself against me, he presses at my entrance, just there, but not...quite...

I wrap my legs around him and arch up toward him. He swears into my mouth and then, like he can't wait any more, he thrusts.

19

Liam

I thrust into Ginny and I've never felt anything so good in my life. She clenches around me and I bury myself deeper. I pull her hips up to me and tilt her so that I can go deeper still. I want more, I want all of her. I grab her mouth and suck on her lips. As I pull on her mouth I draw out of her. The tightness of her wraps around me and I nearly lose it. I push back in. Being inside her. It feels like...I'm home.

I start a rhythm, slow and steady. I want to savor her, let this first time be something we'll never forget.

"You're beautiful," I say. Not just how she looks, but who she is. I take her mouth again and thrust in deep. She cries out and there's a flush on her cheeks and down her chest.

I strum my fingers over her clit.

"Yes," she cries. And as I move, I feel her clench with each little flick over her mound. And each time she clenches, she wraps tighter around me. The world's becoming hazy, there's nothing but us. Her wrapped around me, and me in her. I pull out, push in. I set my forehead against her and look into her eyes. Then I take her hands and lace her fingers through mine.

"I want you," I say.

"I want you, too," she gasps.

"I need you." I say. Her eyes are bright and beautiful.

"I missed you," she says. And the way she says it, like she wishes she could say more, drives me forward. I push into her, touch her everywhere, thrust so deep that I imagine I'm touching her soul. And then, I think I am, because she's crying out and I feel her tightening on me. And I can't stop myself. The only thing I know is that I have to keep going, I can't stop, I have to be inside her. With her always. The pressure builds. My whole body fills with want. The only thing I want in the whole world is to be with her. Right here. Right now.

She arches into me and cries out my name. Then she's grasping me so hard that I can't do anything but what she's telling me to do. The world disappears. It's just her and me. And all I can do is feel her, and empty myself into her, and give her everything I have.

It bursts from me and I shout her name. Spill myself into her. Make her mine. Slowly, her climax reaches its end. She stops pulsing around me and the world comes back into focus. Her eyes look like they reflect the stars, the whole universe. If I could make her look like that every day, my life would be complete.

Gently, I lean down and brush a kiss over her lips.

She reaches up and with quiet tenderness she brushes my jaw with her fingertips.

I roll over onto my back and pull her on top of me. The night air is cool, so I wrap my arms around her and kiss the place where her neck and collarbone meet.

"Okay?" I ask.

She settles her head on my chest. My heart beats against her ear and I rub my fingers lightly over her shoulders.

"Better than okay," she says.

She relaxes against me and we stay quiet listening to the night creatures. I circle my hands over her back and start to wonder how long we can stay like this.

"I was thinking," I say.

"Yeah? Dangerous thing," she says.

"About the future."

She stiffens and I curse myself for broaching this too soon. For spoiling this moment.

"What about it?"

She sits up and goes to her clothes. The dark and her long hair hide her face so I can't see her expression, but her shoulders are tense.

I sit up and pull on my clothes too. It feels wrong, like we're distancing ourselves and putting on armor.

"I thought you and I could..."

Her back is to me, but I see her stiffen even more. "What?"

"Be more than friends." I let the statement hang in the air. She doesn't say anything and she doesn't turn around. "What's wrong? Will you turn around?"

She does, and I wish she hadn't. Because her eyes tell me that she's not interested.

"When are you leaving?"

I look down. "We could do long-distance."

"When?" she asks.

I look up. "Probably in the next week or two."

She nods and clenches her hands. "No thank you."

Her no hits me in the gut. "Why?"

She doesn't answer.

What does she want?

I gesture around. "You want me to stay here? Stay in Centreville forever? What was all this for then? You knew I'd be leaving."

She turns her face away from me. When she looks back the stars in her eyes are gone.

"Why did I train you?" she asks.

"Sure."

"What was this all for?" she asks.

"Yes," I say. Something in me needs to know, needs to hear her say it.

She looks back to the driveway, to the road leading away from here.

"Well. It wasn't for you. And it wasn't for me. Figure it out yourself."

I'm struck by the anguish on her face.

I'm an idiot. It's always been for Bean. None of this was about me. Or us.

"What was this then?" I gesture to the matted down grass. "A thank you fuck? Goodbye?"

She turns away and wraps her arms around herself.

"Sorry. I'm sorry. That was an asshole thing to say."

"No, you're right," she says. "I'm sorry."

We're only standing a few feet apart, but I might as well already be in California.

"Ginny," I say. She looks up at me, and I tell her what I should've started with. "I love you."

She closes her eyes and then wipes at a tear on her face.

"Please don't," she says.

"Why not?"

"Because I can't. I can't depend on you to always be there. And I can't depend on me to make it through."

I go to her. I gather her in my arms and I hold her. She drops her head on my shoulder.

"I don't want this," she says, "I can't be more than friends. Tonight, it was a mistake."

My chest feels like it's cracking open, but I keep holding her.

"Okay," I say. "Alright."

We stand there for a moment longer and I realize this is likely the last time I'll ever hold her. I get where she's coming from. I know her as well as I know myself and I understand. There's only so much one person can carry, and sometimes the thought of sharing that load with another is too scary. So you keep the burden all to yourself. I understand.

"If you ever need me," I say.

"I know," she says.

And that is the end.

We walk back to her car and I hold open her door for her. As she gets in, her phone rings. She pulls it from her pocket.

"It's Enid," she says. "Yes? What? Slow down."

I watch as her face drains of color and she looks at me with growing fear.

"I'll be right there. Call the police. I'm coming."

She hangs up.

"What is it?"

"It's Bean," she says.

And I feel like the world didn't end before, it ended just now.

"She's gone."

20
───────

Ginny

*B*ean's not in her bed. She's not in another room, not in the yard, not at home. She's gone. As soon as Enid told me, a cold fear washed over me and filled me with icy dread. I fight to keep moving so that I can find her. I can't give in to fear because if I do I'll collapse. I know this.

Where is she? Where could she be?

"Bean," I yell. "Bean, where are you? I'm here. Bean?"

I hear Enid calling out "Beatrice?"

And Clark shouting, "Bean?"

Liam runs up to me. His jaw is clenched and he looks scared. Do I look like that? Do I look that scared?

"She's not here," I say.

"No."

We've torn the apartment apart, we've looked in every nook and cranny of house. We've looked everywhere.

"Where could she be," I say.

"The police are coming," he says. But they have to drive over from the county seat, they're at least another thirty minutes away.

I shake my head.

"We'll find her," he says.

I turn on him and the helplessness I feel makes me lash out. "If we hadn't... If I'd gone home when I said I should."

He shakes his head. "No. You can't know."

"Yes." I turn on him. "If I hadn't stayed with you, Bean would be safe. She'd be in bed right now."

He looks as if I punched him. That he doesn't believe what I'm saying. But it's true. It's true.

I turn away from him and jog over to Enid. "Tell me again what happened."

She nods and wipes at her eyes. I've never seen Enid cry, not once in her life. The sight of her tears scares me.

"Enid?"

"Heather came by," she says.

I nod. "Yes."

"Finick ran off after a fight and she couldn't find him. She was worried. Asked if he'd come by."

"And he hadn't."

"No. That boy's been getting into trouble with his friends at the abandoned mill."

"And then what?"

"She was crying. I soothed her. Then I saw Beatrice."

"She was in the doorway?" I can picture her, watching wide-eyed, worrying about her friend Finick.

"That's right. She asked if Finick was okay. I said, laud sakes, child, get back to bed."

"And then, when you checked on her later, she was gone."

Enid's face pinches and she nods.

"Nothing else?"

Enid presses her hands into her eyes, then, she looks back up. "Beatrice said to Heather that she could find Finick because she was...some stuff and nonsense..." She holds up her finger. "Superhawk."

I inhale sharply.

"Skyhawk," says Liam in a low voice.

A chill runs over me. "She went to save him," I say. Bean went out at midnight to save Finick. "The old mill."

I sprint toward my car and Liam runs after me.

~

The old mill is pitch black. It's not been in use for thirty years. I run through the high grass and jump over rusted scrap and rotting logs.

"Do you see anything?" I ask.

Liam runs next to me. He has out his phone and shines the flashlight in front of us. Three tall metal silos rise up in front of us. They look like one-hundred-foot-tall monsters with dark cylindric bodies.

"Bean," I shout. "Finick."

Liam calls out and our voices are swallowed by the eerie quiet of the dilapidated ruin. I keep running. Old, rusted trucks lie on their sides and grass and weeds wrap around them. Liam flashes his light over them and in the dark the rust looks like blood and the metal looks like bones left to rot.

We pass a metal shed. "Look in there," I say.

He passes his flashlight over the graffiti. A door hangs off its hinge and he shoves it aside. I run up behind him and peer over his shoulder. The shed is empty except for broken vodka bottles and a dead rat.

"Nothing," he says.

We turn and keep running toward the silos. They loom over us and I pray that Bean is there, sitting in their shadows, safe with Finick. That we'll find her.

"Bean," I shout again. "Bean, it's Mama. Where are you?"

There's a shriek and I startle. Whip around. Liam shines his flashlight up and an owl dives overhead.

"Bean?"

We make it to the busted and cracked concrete where the grain silos stand. They are so tall. The stairs up are long since broken, they hang off the silos and look like a twisted version of chutes and ladders. I spin in a circle and Liam shines his flashlight through the rubble and the grass.

"Bean? Finick?" I call.

"Finick. Bean."

Nothing. Silence is our answer. Not even the crickets are singing at the old mill tonight.

"They're not here," I say. "She's not here."

Liam's jaw tightens and he shakes his head. "Keep looking—"

"They're not here," I say.

Then we both look up. There was a noise. A scraping sound. Something.

"Did you hear that?" I ask.

He nods.

"Bean?" I call.

"Finick?"

Nothing.

We wait. I hold my breath and strain my ears, pray for a sound, a voice, anything. But finally, I have to breathe again, and when I do, "They're not here. We can go back. Call Enid, see if the police—"

"What was that?"

Then I hear a weak call, a human voice calling from the darkness.

"Bean? Bean, where are you?"

"Up there," says Liam.

He shines his flashlight up the largest grain silo. There, a

hundred feet up I see Finick. His arm hangs over the side and...
he's not moving.

I cry out and run to the silo.

"Ginny, wait," says Liam. "It's not safe."

I look up at the broken stairs, at the twists of metal that in
places hang off the sides. "I don't care," I say.

"Wait for the police. I'll call, get them here."

I can't. There's no way. Finick's not moving. And where's
Bean? Why can't I see her?

"I'm going," I say.

Liam shakes his head. His face goes white. This is his worst
nightmare, come to life.

"I need you," I say. "They need you. Please."

I grab the metal rail of the stairs and start to climb. It rattles
and swings under my weight. My heart pounds and I taste the
metal tang of fear in my mouth. Still, I climb as quickly as I can
without putting too much pressure on the groaning stairs. But
then the sharp shriek of metal sounds and the section of stairs
I'm standing on swings away from the silo. I scream and grab
the rail with both hands.

The rust fragments bite into my skin and I start to slip. The
stairs groan again, shake and I'm dislodged from the rail. The
breath knocks out of me. I'm twenty feet above the ground and
in free fall. I can't breathe to scream. I can't...I'm not...I can't
save Bean.

It's a millisecond but a thousand thoughts flash in my mind.
I've failed. I'm falling, the stairs twist around me, I'm falling and
I've let my daughter down. I can't save her. I never could save
her. She's hurt and sick and I can't save her. And now, I'm
falling and when I hit the ground I might die. I might not
survive to see her again. And I love her so much. I love her with
everything that I am. But I've failed. In my mind, I see George,
he's swimming down through the black water, coming back to
me, to save Bean, to save me. Is this how he felt? Like it didn't

matter if he didn't survive, because more than anything he had to save us? His face lights above me, I reach up to him. "I can't save her," I say. "I can't save our baby."

"You don't have to," he says. "It's okay. You're okay. Let go."

"I can't."

"Let go," he says.

"I'm sorry," I say. "I failed."

"I love you. Both of you," he says.

Then he's gone and I'm alone. And instead of being pulled to the surface, I'm falling. It's all done.

The millisecond passes, the rest of my life flashes before my eyes, and the one thing I see, the one thing I see that I wish I'd seen before was that I didn't have to do it alone. I could've let go, shared the burden.

Not just on a superficial level, where I kept parts of myself back, but all the way. I should've trusted. I should've let him help me. I should've let him love me.

Liam.

I wish I'd told him the truth. That I love him too.

But now, instead of hearing that, he gets to see me fall.

To hit the ground.

He gets to relive his worst nightmare, except this time, he has to watch it happen. Which, I think, is a thousand times worse. Watching someone you love get hurt and not being able to stop it is the worst pain in the world.

21

Liam

Ginny climbs up onto the stairs and the panic that consumes me when I think of flying, of falling, starts to scrape along my insides. I drag in a breath. I can do this. The panic clenches at my throat and presses down on my chest. I blink as my vision goes in and out. The memory of my spine crunching against concrete clashes around my skull.

I drag in a deep breath, beat back the panic. Ginny's already ten feet up. She's going without me. To save Bean. To get Finick.

I look up at Finick's arm, hanging over the edge of the silo, at least a hundred feet up. Dizziness. I stumble.

"Do this," I say. "You can do this."

The panic is there, a beast waiting to consume me. Keep me here, planted on the ground. Safe in its grasp. For years I've run from it. Fought it. Retreated from the world. Nothing I did worked, not therapy, not medication, nothing. I look up at Ginny, she grasps the railing and inches along the stairs. They groan.

Be a hero.

"Shit," I say.

Be a hero.

She needs you. They need you.

There's nothing in this life I want more than to be with Ginny and Bean. Be someone they can depend on. Be more than a hero. Be their family.

This time when the panic grips me, I don't fight it. I don't struggle against it. I invite the monster in. I open myself wide.

It rushes in, takes over. The fear, the pounding heart, the terror, the falling sensation, the knowledge that *I'm going to die right now* grips me. Twists me. I can't breathe.

More, I tell it.

My body goes cold then hot.

More.

I can't breathe.

More. Do your worst.

I open myself to it, I let it ravage inside me, and I don't fight it. I let all of the terror, fear, panic fill me and I surrender to it.

Just let it be. Acknowledge it. Accept it.

And then, I run.

I sprint toward the stairs and pull myself up. All the training, all the running, every minute of physical training I've done has been preparing me for this moment.

The stairs swing wide and I grab a ledge and pull myself up higher. Ginny's only ten feet above me. I take the stairs as fast as I can.

I look up, and see what Ginny doesn't. The section above her has pulled loose from the silo. Most of the bolts are missing. When she runs onto it the metal screeches angrily. My blood runs cold. The stairs yank away from the wall. She grabs the railing, starts to fall. Her legs fly up in the air. The stairs fall and Ginny's falling with them.

I don't think. I run as fast as I can. Sprint up the stairs. Leap toward her, and as she passes through the air. I dive forward. I grasp my railing with one hand, leap over the edge and grab her wrist.

She's still hanging onto the railing of the dangling stairs.

Her eyes are closed.

"Let go," I say. I grit my teeth. I'm hanging from the stairs, holding her up with one hand.

"I can't," she says.

"Let go." I say.

Then, the stairs she's on falls away completely. And she's not letting go and I can't hold her.

"Let go," I shout.

The stairs fall out of her grasp. She screams.

Her hand slips from mine. She starts to fall.

I can't let her. I won't. I grab her fingers, and hang on with everything I have.

Slowly, I pull her up, until she can grab the stairs on her own. She drags herself over the edge and I swing my arm over and pull myself up too.

I collapse against the metal and draw in a long breath. Below us, the stairs lie on the concrete in a twisted wreck.

Ginny looks at me. Her expression stunned. She's breathing hard and her hands are cut and bloody.

"You came," she says. "You saved me."

A lump lodges in my throat. I nod.

She launches into my arms and wraps her arms around me. "I love you," she whispers. "I'm sorry I never told you. I'm sorry. I love you."

I pull back. "It's okay," I say. "I know. I love you too."

I look up at the silo. Bean and Finick are still up there. Fifteen feet of stairs have pulled away. There's no way up except to scale the wall, using the grooves and the bolts from the pulled-away stairs as hand holds.

"I'm going up."

"I'll come," she says.

I shake my head. "Look at your hands. You won't make it."

She presses a warm kiss against my lips. "I love you," she says.

I take in her face and the love that she's giving me. It makes me strong.

I've rock climbed before. In my movies, I was constantly scaling skyscrapers, but every time I was in a harness. This time, there's no fail safe. One wrong move...

It doesn't matter.

I look up at the sheer wall and the tiny handholds. I kick off my shoes and socks and wipe my palms off on my jeans. Then I turn and pull myself up onto the side of the silo.

I move up the wall and steadily work my way higher. I pinch my fingers into grooves and squeeze my feet onto inch wide bolts. My muscles start to shake and I send a thanks to Ginny and her boot camp hell. I couldn't have done this otherwise. My hands and feet are cut up as I work them into tiny holds and over rusted bolts and half-inch-wide ledges. When they get too sticky with blood, I pause my upward progress and wipe them off on my pants. Finally, I make it to the next stretch of stairs. I check the bolts. It looks intact. I set my palms on the base and pull myself up. The metal groans but holds.

I climb the steps. At the next segment, I check the integrity of the metal, then step up. I twist around the silo, and climb as fast as I can. I look down to the ground, and far below, in the darkness I can see Ginny watching.

Then I'm at the top. I vault myself over the railing and land.

When I see them, my heart stops. I nearly fall to my knees.

I run forward.

Finick's unconscious. Bean's superhero cape is rolled into a bandage and tied in a tight knot around his thigh. Blood soaks it. He's pale and breathing shallowly.

Bean lies next to him. I can't see anything wrong with her.

But when I call her name she won't wake up. Her pulse is steady, but...she won't wake up.

The next five minutes, while I check Bean's pulse, over and over, and press on Finick's thigh, those five minutes are the longest of my life.

22

Ginny

*W*e're at the children's hospital in Bean's room.
Liam, Enid, Clark, Heather, Joel, Redge,
Finick. Everyone's here. It's been twenty hours and she still
hasn't woken up. The heart monitor keeps up a steady beat, and
I don't know whether I love it for saying she's still here with us,
or hate it, because she has to be on it. The doctor's said that the
physical and emotional stress of "the event" caused this. That it
was too much in her weakened state.

"Drink some coffee," says Enid.

She hands me a Styrofoam cup full of black hospital sludge.
I shake my head. I don't want it. Enid sighs and sets it on the
bedside table. The room is small, maybe ten by ten, and with
eight of us in here, it's near bursting. The high emotions in the
room are almost too much for me. I just want everyone to go so
I can lay on the bed and cuddle my baby.

I reach down and take her hand. It's limp in mine.

"This is your fault," Enid says. The anger in her voice cuts through the depressed atmosphere.

I look up, because I figure she's talking to Liam and she's about to unleash her mountain of misery lecture. But she's not. She's looking at Heather.

Heather makes a rude noise and glares. "It is not. I'm not the fool that encouraged her daughter to become a superhero."

"Stuff it, Heather. Bean saved my life," says Finick. He says he would've bled out if she hadn't come.

"If you didn't hang out with those *friends*, then this wouldn't have happened. If it's anyone's fault it's yours."

When Finick went to the old mill he and his friends decided to climb the silo and throw their knives. One of them accidentally hit Finick in the thigh. Then, when he started to bleed and passed out, they left him. Bean got there just in time to see them running away.

"Yeah. Fine. It's my fault," says Finick. "According to you, everything's my fault."

"Quiet, boy. You're lucky your sister took you in," says Joel.

I look at Liam and try to gather some calm from him. How is this helping? Who cares whose fault it is?

"I'm not talking about tonight," says Enid. "I mean all of this." She gestures at me, at Bean on the bed, at Finick. "It's your fault, Heather. Daughter of my heart or not. You need to stop."

Heather's eyes flick from me to Bean and away again.

"He left because of you. You weren't good for him," Enid says.

The air grows thick and full of old pain. Joel looks between Enid and Heather, confused and wary. Finick tilts his head and watches Heather.

"Who left? Me?" asks Finick.

Silence fills the space with tension, everyone watches

Heather. Then, she looks up at me and her eyes are filled with resolve.

She turns to Finick. "Not you," Heather says. "Your father."

"My father?" asks Finick.

"George."

The room erupts with noise. I look between Finick and Heather, Bean and Finick, Finick and...Finick is Bean's brother?

Finick's father is George?

"Does that mean...are you..." asks Finick. *My mother* hangs in the air, unsaid.

"She darned well better not be," says Joel. He looks at Finick with disgust. "Good for nothing."

Finick's face turns white.

"What a loser," says Redge. "The son of a dead guy."

Clark slaps his hand against the tray table and a potted flower flips to the floor and shatters.

"Get out," he says. He points at Redge.

"Hey now," says Joel. "He's just expressing an opinion."

Clark rounds on Joel and points an angry finger at him. "You too. Get out. My son was a good man. You shame his memory. Get out."

Joel looks around in shock. But Clark stands his ground. Finally, he grabs Redge's arm and pulls him out of the room. "Come on, Heather. Finick," he says. He waits at the door.

Heather looks at Bean, then shakes her head no. Finick doesn't look Joel's way.

"Heather?"

"I'll be out in a minute," she says.

Joel gives her a black look then leaves.

"How did you know?" asks Heather. She's watching Enid's pinched face.

"He looks just like George as a teenager. Likes the same food, the same sweets. And his voice, when it went deep, it's just the same. I didn't know before then. Only suspected until now."

Heather nods, accepting this.

"I'm...you're not my sister?" Finick asks.

Heather won't look at him. "No."

"You're my mom," he says. Heather flinches and curves in on herself. He turns to Enid. "You're my grandma."

Enid nods. "Yes."

He looks at Clark. "And you're my grandpa."

"Guess so," says Clark. "Didn't expect to gain a grandson today."

Finick smiles at this.

Liam has a curious look on his face. Then he turns to Heather. "You were never an actress. You were never in any movies."

I don't understand what that has to do with anything.

Heather nods. "It was our story," she says. "I was young. I didn't want it. The pregnancy."

Finick stiffens and I ache to reach out to him.

"My parents convinced me that we could all go away for a year. Then they'd take the baby and pretend it was their late life miracle." She shrugs. "My short acting career was our story."

"I'm Bean's brother," says Finick. His eyes fill with wonder. And my heart fills with wonder too. "Why didn't you tell me?" he asks.

Heather turns away from him and wipes her eyes. "I was scared," she says. "And I hated that he chose her over me." She looks up at me and her eyes are red. "I wanted you to hurt."

Liam moves to stand in front of me.

"Mountains of misery," says Enid. "That's you, Heather Wilson. A steaming pile of misery."

"I'm sorry," she says to me. "I'm sorry for what I've done."

She kept Finick from Bean.

"I'm Bean's brother," says Finick again.

He looks at me and I nod.

"You have a sister," I say. I squeeze Bean's hand. "You've got a brother," I tell her.

"I could save her," Finick says. He turns back to Heather. "You were going to let her die without me trying to save her?"

She flinches.

"I wouldn't have. I would've said something. I was going to..."

Finick steps up and stands next to Bean. "I'm going to see if I'm a match. I want to be her donor. She saved me. Now I can save her."

But he's a half-brother, and the chances of him being a match are slim to none.

Still, he wants to try.

I pray for a miracle.

I pray with my whole heart. For the long wait while Finick is tested, I pray, and bargain and think of a thousand things I'll do or give if only...

The miracle doesn't come.

Finick isn't a match.

23

Liam

Finick isn't a match. When we get the news, I watch the light of hope that was shining in Ginny flicker and then die.

Bean's woken up a few times in the past few days, but she's in pain and she quickly falls back asleep. We're getting to the point where even a transplant won't help.

"It's okay," Ginny says to Finick. "You tried." She gives him a hug. He squeezes her back. When she lets him go, he turns aside so that Ginny can't see when he quickly wipes at his eyes.

"We're going to head out," says Heather. "We have to get settled at Enid and Clark's."

"Why?" asks Ginny. I can tell she's surprised.

"Joel wants a divorce." Heather looks down at her feet. I realize she's no longer in her usual designer dresses and heels, she's in a sundress and flip-flops. She looks different. Kinder.

"I'm sorry," says Ginny, and I realize...she means it. She and

Heather have talked over the past few days, they must've come to an understanding.

Heather shrugs. "I guess it's time I started living life differently. I was doing it wrong. I wasn't very nice."

"Yeah," says Finick.

Heather looks at the ceiling. "Can't argue with the truth," she says.

"Come on, *Mom*," says Finick.

Heather rolls her eyes. "Let me know, if you need anything. Real coffee. Food."

"Don't expect the niceness to last," says Finick.

"Bye," says Ginny.

They wave and we're quiet as they walk out of the hospital room.

I look back at Bean. She's so small and fragile under the blanket, with IVs hooked into her and machines all around. I didn't realize how small she was. When she was awake, she was so vibrant and full of life that it was hard to remember she's a six-year-old with a rare childhood leukemia in dire need of a bone marrow transplant.

Ginny settles down on the bed by Bean and I pull up a chair next to her. I rub my hand in circles over her arm and try to lend her a bit of strength.

Ginny gives me a soft smile. "Thanks for being here."

I look down at her in surprise. "Where else would I be?"

"I don't know. Hollywood?"

"Not a chance."

"Finick told me you got the role. I'm proud of you."

My agent called this morning. I've been offered a contract for another three movies in the Liam Stone movie franchise. Right now, that's the last thing on my mind.

Ginny's eyes flicker to the TV screen hanging from the far wall. It's on and a commercial has started.

"That's you," says Ginny.

She grabs the remote and turns up the volume. She watches in amazement as I tell the world about a special little girl I care about who desperately needs a transplant. She sits up in bed and leans toward the television.

The commercial is coming to an end and the camera zooms in.

"You don't need to be a superhero to save someone's life," I say in the commercial. "You can be a hero by registering for the bone marrow transplant list. Please do so today."

The commercial ends. Ginny fumbles with the remote. Her hand shakes and she turns the TV off. Then she looks over at me. She reaches out and touches her fingers to my heart. Her fingers tremble on my chest.

"You did this for...for Bean?"

I swallow and nod.

"When?" she asks.

"The week I went to LA."

"You went there for this?"

Her hand burns on my chest and my heart pounds. "I thought it might help, that someone would see it and be the one."

A single tear trails down her cheek.

I reach up and wipe it away. "Don't cry," I say. "I'm sorry if it was the wrong thing. I didn't want to tell you. In case it failed."

She half sobs, half laughs at my excuse.

"That sounds familiar," she says. And I remember her saying the same thing to me about pursuing her degree. She didn't want anyone to know in case she failed.

"I...are you okay?" I ask.

"You weren't in LA, planning to leave us. You were there for Bean."

I nod.

"Not for movies or auditions or..."

"You're my family," I say. "You come first."

She purses her lips together, trying to keep in the tears.

"I don't care if you don't want to marry me. If you're not looking for a husband, or for a substitute father, or for anything more than friends. You're still my family, I'll do anything for you. I'll be there for you. Always."

Her hand splays over my chest and she reaches up with her other hand to cup her fingers against my cheek.

"I love you," she whispers.

My heart cracks open under her hands and fills my chest with warmth.

"You're my family, too," she says.

"Always?" I ask.

"And forever." She leans forward and presses a soft kiss to my lips.

"And Bean?" I ask.

"She adopted you the minute she met you," Ginny says.

"I'm here for you. I'll be here, for it all. And after," I say. "No matter what happens. You can depend on me."

Ginny looks at me and I wonder what she's thinking, but then she says, "I know. I trust you."

I gather her in my arms and hold her to me.

When we finally pull apart I hear a doctor clear his throat from the doorway.

"Mrs. Weaver?"

"Yes?" says Ginny. Her voice is wary.

My stomach drops. What is it? "Is something wrong?" I ask.

The doctor shakes his head then smiles. "We've found a donor. That commercial you did that's been playing for weeks. It worked."

I look at Ginny and what the doctor says finally sinks in, because she bursts into tears. I wrap her in my arms.

24

Ginny

I love heroes. Everything about them. Their strength, their honor, their devotion, their pursuit of the ultimate goal in the face of unsurmountable odds. A hero always does what's right, always wins, no matter what.

Okay, scratch that. I have a new definition of a hero. A hero tries, a hero gives, a hero loves. Like Finick said, anybody can be a hero. You just have to be willing to do something selfless.

I reach over and put my hand on top of Liam's. He looks over at me and his eyes crinkle in the early spring sunlight.

"Almost there," he says. He gives me that smile, the one that's only for me, and my chest feels ready to burst it's so full of happiness.

I glance to the backseat of the car. Bean's strapped in her car seat. She has a pile of comic books in her lap. It's been more than eight months since we found her donor. It was a long, hard climb, but she made it. We did it. Bean's cheeks are pink, her short hair is curly, and she's put her baby fat back on. She has a healthy, happy glow that makes my heart sing.

Liam started filming his latest movie last month, and Bean can't wait to go to the premier in her Skyhawk costume. She's one lucky kid.

Her nose is buried in a comic book and I'm struck with a wave of nostalgia. We bump down a washed out dirt road. We're ten miles outside of Centreville where Route 511 crosses Route 511B and turns onto Pine Tree Road. Liam turns onto the long drive up his property. There's a brand new wood fence along the drive, painted white, with daffodils blooming at the base.

Bean puts down her comic and leans forward in her seat.

"Is it a secret base?" she asks.

"It's a surprise," says Liam.

"Or an airplane?"

"It's a surprise," says Liam.

"Or a superhero training camp, with climbing walls and zip lines and—"

"It's a—"

"Surprise," she says.

I laugh.

"Or maybe it's a wellness center for Mama. Cause she's graduated now."

I turn around and wink at Bean. We celebrated my graduation with my degree in Sports Medicine last week. But I know that it isn't a wellness center because we've already leased a building in downtown Centreville.

Liam looks back and grins at Bean. "It's a surprise."

She groans, but she doesn't have to wait long. The trees open before us and I gasp.

The trailer's gone. The weeds are gone. It's all gone.

Instead.

"It *is* a secret base," cries Bean.

Liam laughs. We pull up the circular drive and Liam parks the car. Bean jumps out and runs down the cobblestone path. I step out after her and Liam comes around to me.

"What do you think?" he asks. He seems worried that I might not like it. How could I not?

I look up. It's a huge log home, with tall windows, a two-story stone fireplace, lush gardens full of spring blooms, a wide wooden deck. The sun shines down on us and the sound of birds chirping fills the air.

"It's a home," I say.

He nods and he smiles at the awestruck expression on my face. "It's a home."

Then he drops down on one knee and takes my hands in his. "I love you," he says. "I don't want to wait another day. Will you marry me? Will you give me the honor of being yours for the rest of our lives."

I look into his eyes and the only thing I can see is the man I love.

"Yes, yes," I say.

He stands up and pulls me into him. Captures my mouth in a searing kiss. He spins me around, and I'm laughing and crying and kissing him when Bean runs up to us.

"Mama, Mama," she says.

Liam sets me down. Bean pulls on my shirt.

"Mama. Grandma's out back and Grandpa, and Heather and Finick, and even Redge. And Grandma said Redge is a mountain of misery, and then Finick said tell me about it, and Grandpa said I could eat all the cake I wanted, but I had to wait until after—"

Her hand flies to cover her mouth and her eyes go wide.

"After what?" I ask.

I look at Liam. He's having a hard time containing his smile.

"After what, Bean?"

Then Bean starts to jump up and down.

Liam clears his throat. "After the wedding," he says. "If you'll do me the honor."

"'Cause Grandma says you can't live in a house together without being married, 'cause that's heathen and only misery and tarnation come with that."

Liam laughs and winks at me. We've been doing a lot of heathen, I guess.

Then, all the people I love come around from the side of the house. They're in tuxes and fancy dresses. And it turns out, we don't just have a beautiful home fit for a family, we have a wedding, and it's taking place today.

"We got dresses, Mama. I'm the flower girl, and you're the bride. And Grandma says we're gonna look so pretty." Then she stops, and stares up at me, eyes wide. "Mama?"

"Yes?"

"I'm so happy," she says.

I smile down at her, then at Liam. "Me too."

"And we're gonna always be happy," she says.

"That's right," I say. "Because we're a family."

Liam looks at me with so much love in his eyes that I can barely hold all the joy inside.

"And family is the best superpower of all," he says.

I take Bean and Liam's hands, and we go together, hearts full of joy, walking into our future.

HE END

JOIN SARAH READY'S NEWSLETTER

Want more Ginny and Liam? Get an exclusive epilogue and bonus scenes from *Hero Ever After* for newsletter subscribers only.

When you join the Sarah Ready Newsletter you get access to sneak peaks, insider updates, exclusive bonus scenes, bonus epilogues and more.

Join Today!

www.sarahready.com/newsletter

ABOUT THE AUTHOR

Sarah Ready is the author of *The Fall in Love Checklist* and *Hero Ever After*. She writes contemporary romance, romantic comedy and women's fiction. You can find her online at www. sarahready.com.

ALSO BY SARAH READY

The Fall in Love Checklist

Chasing Romeo (May, 2021)

Find more books by Sarah Ready at:

www.sarahready.com/romance-books

Made in United States
Troutdale, OR
08/05/2023

11810740R00105